Full Moon Howl

By

Orlando A. Sanchez

A Montague & Strong Detective Novel

There are nights when the wolves are silent and the moon howls.-George Carlin

Published by OM Publishing NY NY

Cover Design by Deranged Doctor Design
www.derangeddoctordesign.com

ONE

"SHE TOLD ME you could help me. I need to stop this tonight—before the change," he pleaded as he gripped the edge of the conference table. "Before I hurt someone else."

I opened my mouth to speak and immediately regretted it. The stench wafting across the table sucker-punched me, forcing me to grimace as I held my breath. The smell hung on him—a shroud of illness that filled the room. Part of me wished Charon would stroll through the door or wall at any second and claim him, just to clear the air.

The other part of me realized we were dealing with a real threat. A sick Were was a dangerous Were. The snuffling and rumbling from under the table told me Peaches was having a hard time breathing too. Only Monty seemed immune to the putrid miasma crawling across the room. If he smelled anything, his sense of propriety would never let him outwardly display it. He was English, after all.

Douglas Bishop, our Were client, was a nervous, thin man of medium height. His pale skin glistened in the waning rays of sunlight that crept through the window. A worn gray suit, a few sizes too large, draped loosely over his body. He completed the ensemble with a sweat-stained off-white shirt and dark tie.

He'd let go of the conference table and his hands were clasped tightly before him. He would clench them into fists after every sentence, followed by pushing his glasses up the bridge of his nose. Yes, it was driving me crazy. A pair of silver restraints sat next to him on the table. I had silver ammo in Grim Whisper, and Monty as backup. Better to have it and not need it than the alternative.

"You have to do this—before the change," he pleaded again. "You have to reverse this."

"Lycanthropy is irreversible. It can't be undone,"

Monty said, flexing his fingers. "Weren't you informed of this?"

"Then kill me, before I hurt someone else," Douglas pleaded. "Please." His body seized and he coughed uncontrollably. It was a wet sound that went on for nearly half a minute.

"Do you want some water?" I asked, but he waved me away and managed to get himself under control.

"We have plenty of pests in this office, but we are not an extermination service," Monty said, his voice hard, as he turned to look at me.

"You have to help me," Douglas said as a shiver passed over his body. "I can't go out. I'm not safe—no one is safe."

"When did you first realize you were ill?" I asked through shallow breaths. "How long have you been like this?"

"Since last week," he said, and coughed again, hacking a glob of phlegm onto the conference table.

My stomach clenched and I resisted the urge to revisit my lunch.

"I'm sorry," Douglas said while wiping the phlegm with his sleeve, which only smeared it across the table. "I can't control it."

"This is what we get for listening to that vampire of yours, Simon," Monty muttered. I watched as he stood up and retrieved the disinfectant and a cloth.

"If Chi sent him, it's important," I said, taking my hands off the table. "By the way, what do you mean 'before the change'? It's not a full moon tonight."

"Doesn't matter. I've been changing every night since I felt like this. Don't need a full moon."

"You're changing without a full moon? Only a very old and powerful Were can do that," Monty answered, cleaning the table. "And you're neither. This may have a deeper source. I don't think it's just some Were illness."

"Douglas, have you tried going to the Dark Council?" I asked. "They really are equipped to deal with this sort of thing."

"The Dark Council told me they couldn't help me!" he yelled, pounding the table. "I saw them yesterday and they said it was hopeless, that I should just end it or have someone do it for me."

A low rumble crept along the floor from under the table.

"Douglas, I need you to calm down," I said, glancing at Peaches, "and I mean *now*."

He took a deep breath and sat back in his chair. I looked under the table again. Peaches was no longer sprawled, but rested on his stomach and focused on Douglas. He gave me a quick look as if to say "Can I have him for lunch?" I shook my head and he dropped his, clearly disappointed.

"Sometimes the body can't resist the turning and it has an adverse reaction," Monty said, moving to the other side of the table. "Although I haven't seen anything this severe. Have you been exposed to any strange magic?"

"You don't understand," Douglas said, and I saw him convulse. "I can't control it. Once I turn, I'm a threat—a menace to anyone around me."

"I get it, and right now turning is not a good idea," I said, pushing my chair back. "Let's think some calm thoughts and see if we can solve this."

"It's too late, it's happening." He clenched his teeth as he gripped the table. "You need to run. Get away while you can."

I reached for the silver restraints that were still on the table and attempted to put them on his wrists. I managed to get one on him and I received a hairy back-fist in return. I slid down the conference table and over the end.

I got to my feet and saw Douglas convulse again as his body shifted and began the transformation. The restraint had no effect. He shredded his oversized suit and went full-Werewolf.

"Monty, the restraint isn't stopping the turn. Are you sure it isn't a full moon? You didn't schedule to meet a sick Were during a full moon, did you?"

"No," Monty answered as he stepped back. "I wouldn't have scheduled this meeting on a full moon, Simon. This is a forced change and looks like dark magic."

"Well, *he* didn't get the memo," I pointed at Douglas as he turned. "And what do you mean 'dark magic'? He's a Were, not a sorcerer."

I didn't want to shoot Douglas. He seemed like a nice person and had come to us for help. The Werewolf he transformed into, however—not so nice.

The smell intensified with the transformation, which I didn't think was possible. It was now an essence of wet dog with a side of vomit. His bloodshot eyes fixed on me and he snarled. Peaches answered with a growl of his own.

"Hello, Tristan," Werewolf Douglas rasped. "It really has been too long."

"It's for you," I said as I moved back. "You know him?"

"I've never met him before today. Who sent you?"

"Looks like he knows you." I shrugged.

"Oh, I do," Douglas said with a snarl. "I'm coming and I'm bringing hell with me, Tristan."

"Much better in *Tombstone* when Kurt Russell said it," I answered. "Why don't you de-wolf and we can speak like civilized creatures?"

"I have a message for you, mage," Douglas said and raked a claw across the conference table—the very expensive mahogany conference table. Monty clenched his jaw, flexed his hands, and narrowed his eyes as he looked down at the marks.

I looked too and saw that the claw marks were a design. It reminded me of crude Nazca lines. This one looked like a bird with wings outstretched.

"Whom shall I say is delivering this message?" Monty asked, his voice grim. "Do you have a name?"

"I'm going to start with the Weres first and then I'm going to erase all of the abominations," Douglas rasped and coughed up more phlegm. "I'll leave you and the golden mages for last, old friend."

I tried to breathe through my mouth and not gag. "I have a message for you, Doug—bath…posthaste. Seriously, the reekage is strong with this one, Monty."

"Do I know you?" Monty asked again as Peaches bounded out from under the table and lunged at Douglas. Douglas backhanded the dog across the room, which only made him angrier as he stalked back. Peaches, an offspring of Cerberus, was not your average hound.

Douglas jumped over the table and landed next to me. He raked his claws across my chest and got my attention in a hurry. Monty hit him with an orb of air, which punched into his chest and turned him around. He recovered fast enough to impale my arm with his other hand. He pulled me close and nearly knocked me unconscious with his breath.

"Douglas, would a mint be asking too much—ahh—?" I said as he squeezed his claws into my arm and pulled my face close to his. His bloodshot eyes gazed into mine as drool escaped the side of his mouth.

"Behold, I am coming quickly and my reward is with me, to give to each according to what he has done. I am the Alpha and the Omega, the First and the Last, the Beginning and the End." He then tossed me across the room.

I managed to twist my body midair and caught a glimpse of him closing on me. I pulled out Grim Whisper and fired twice as I landed on my back. The rounds hit him square in the chest. The effect was immediate. He transformed back into human form and died several seconds later.

"Shit, Monty," I said, angry. "I didn't want to kill him. The restraint didn't work. Why didn't it work?"

"I don't know." Monty removed the restraint to inspect it. "These restraints are designed to negate a Were turning. I've never seen them fail."

"I hate that I had to shoot him, but he didn't look like he was getting closer to chatting."

The claw marks on my chest and arm burned and itched as they started to heal. My immunity to magic extended to vampires trying to drain me and

Werewolves intent on removing parts of my body. Still hurt like hell, though. I looked down at my ruined shirt and cursed.

"This was a Balmain, Monty," I said, pointing at my shirt. "I'm out a shirt thanks to a psycho Werewolf."

"He was unwell," Monty answered, sounding pensive.

"Is that what you're calling unwell? He was *infected*. Like the other Were we chased down in the Village."

"I'm more concerned about the messages. That pattern of speech sounded familiar."

"If the restraint had worked, we could've asked him," I said, looking at Douglas's lifeless body. "I'd better call Allen. A dead Were is bad news."

"You had no choice, but you will have to explain this to the Dark Council, and your vampire."

"I know. I don't think she'll be pleased. The last part, that quote—the one he recited, I've heard it before. Sounded biblical."

"Revelation 22:12, 13," Monty said, rubbing his chin. "Speaks of the second coming of Christ, according to the Bible."

"Douglas was being controlled by the Messiah?" I shook my head. "Somehow I doubt that."

"I don't recall ever reading where he was a Werewolf," Monty replied. "At least not in *my* studies."

"Then that means someone who can turn a Werewolf without a full moon is coming to pay us a visit."

"Sounds like an impending catastrophe," Monty answered and made his way to the kitchen.

"Is there another kind?" I asked, holstering Grim

Whisper and pulling out my phone.

"No," he said. "I'd better make some tea."

TWO

The knock at the door was strong enough to convince me that someone was barely holding back from ripping it from its hinges. I heard some rapid cursing in Japanese and then another earth-shattering knock.

"Simon, open the door. This is urgent."

It was Michiko.

Yama, recognizing the voice, moved to get to the door and was stopped in his tracks by Peaches. The growl rumbling from his chest sounded like the subway had diverted to run underneath the apartment. Peaches had materialized in the center of the reception area, hackles raised and eyes fixed on the door.

Monty had casually entered the room with a faint smile on his face.

"This should be interesting," he said as he leaned against the doorframe, holding a cup of tea. "Don't you want to let her in?"

"Seriously reconsidering at the moment," I replied, giving him a look. "She doesn't sound like she's in a good mood."

Another wrecking-ball knock caused some of the dust to float down from the ceiling. Yama stood frozen, looking at Peaches. Georgianna opened the darkroom door and took it all in.

"Come here, boy," she said groggily.

Peaches ignored her.

"Sounds like your vampire wants to come in," Monty said after a sip. "Rude to keep her waiting."

"Why isn't she *inside* already? She never knocks."

"Simon, I see you finally took my advice and heightened your security," Michiko said, followed by another rapid string of Japanese cursing. "Open the door now, before I destroy it."

"Shit. Monty, can you move Peaches?"

He shook his head and smiled again.

"I need some biscuits," he said, casually making his way to the kitchen.

"Biscuits. Really? Did you hear what I just said? Are you not seeing the potential disaster here?"

"He's your dog, remember?" he said from the kitchen. "I didn't bond with him—you did. Besides, how exactly do you suggest I move him? Fireball?"

I looked at the concentrated fury of fur in the middle of the floor.

"Stay," I said in my most commanding Darth voice and pointed at him. Peaches didn't react or even acknowledge me. He just kept his eyes fixed forward on the door. "A fireball may not be such a bad idea."

I walked over, unlocked the door, and opened it a crack.

"Hello, Chi," I said with a smile. "Good to see you."

"What are you doing? Open it," she said and placed a hand on the door.

"Not such a good idea. How can I help you?"

"You can help me by opening the door."

I noticed movement out of the corner of my eye. I turned my head to see Monty move Yama and

Georgianna to one side of the room. He waved me on to continue dealing with Chi.

"We have a bit of a situation. Maybe I can meet you later?"

"You did *not* just say that," she whispered, slowly retracting her hand from the door. "'Meet you later'? I don't have time for this."

"Shite, duck!" I heard Monty yell as the door flew off the hinges and sailed across the room, taking me with it.

A cushion of air caught me as I landed, sprawled out, on the floor next to the door. Thanks to Monty, I hadn't ended up crushed to a pulp under it.

"You knew she was going to overreact," I said as I stood up. "So glad this is humorous to you."

"You have no idea," he said around a smile. "Better warn her."

He pointed to the entrance with his chin.

"Chi, wait," I said, holding up a hand. "Don't move."

She stood transfixed at the threshold. Her eyes were locked with Peaches.

"We need to talk," she said, never taking her eyes off the larger-than-natural dog-like creature standing statuesque and growling at her from the middle of the floor. "What the hell is that?"

"*That* is Peaches," I said.

"And our new security system," Monty added, taking another sip. "Quite effective, I might add. He's the reason you're out *there* instead of in here."

"Mage,"—she narrowed eyes at Monty—"this was your idea, wasn't it?"

Monty pointed at me with a biscuit.

"That's Simon's new pet," he said, staring back at her. "He's bonded to it, not I, and if I recall correctly, heightened security was *your* idea."

She pressed her lips together, crossed her arms, and stared at me. She wore a black-and-red blouse with black leggings covered by a long black coat. Her hair was in a loose bun with a pair of long steel hairpins.

"Well?" she asked, still staring at me.

"Well what?" I was completely confused. "Did I miss something? Come in?"

"If she tries to cross the threshold, it will get ugly," Monty said. "You have to extend—"

"You have to extend your bond to me or else he will attack," she said. "I have no wish to kill your runed guard dog."

I looked at Monty, who nodded and was thoroughly enjoying himself. I would spike his tea later—my revenge would be bitter and its name was *coffee*.

"How do I do that? It's not like he came with an instruction manual."

"Take her hand and place the other on his head, right above the eyes," Monty instructed. "Use your marked hand to touch him."

I took Chi's hand and placed my left hand on Peaches' forehead.

"She's okay, boy," I whispered, and really hoped he understood. "She's a friend."

He stopped rumbling and then…disappeared.

"Where is he?" she asked, stepping past the threshold.

"Who? Peaches?" I craned my neck, and looking to the rear of the space. "Probably the conference room."

"No, not that thing you call a dog," she said, waving my words away. "Where is the Werewolf I sent to you today? I need to have some words with him."

"What's going on?" I asked, concerned.

Something had her rattled. This meant whatever or whoever it was, it was powerful and lethal.

"We have a problem and he may be the only one who has the answer."

"He's dead," I said, and stepped back when she twisted my way suddenly. My hand reflexively moved to the hilt of Ebonsoul. Her eyes flicked down at the movement.

"*You* killed him?" She slowly looked from me to Monty. "Which one of you killed him?"

"I did," I said, keeping my hand on Ebonsoul since she was acting more menacing than usual. "Why?"

"He gave us no choice," Monty said. "He turned without a full moon and attacked."

"*Chikusho.* Without a moon?" she said under her breath, looking around. "Where's the body?"

I pointed to the back of the office. "Conference room." "Why? What's wrong? I called Allen to come get the body."

She was already moving. "Did he scratch or bite anyone?" Her voice was full of urgency.

We entered the conference room to the earlier stench on steroids. My nose shut down and my eyes began to water.

"What the hell?" I gasped and stepped back until I could breathe again. Monty and Chi both entered the room.

"You didn't answer my question," she said as she

examined Douglas' body.

I shook my head. "He was pretty focused on me when he turned," I said, showing her my shredded shirt.

"Did he attack anyone besides you? The mage or Yama?"

"Thank you for the concern, but no, just me and my limited-edition Balmain."

She turned the body over with a foot. "You are immune to vampire and Werewolf attacks. Worrying about you would be a pointless exercise."

"I'm touched," I said, leaning forward to look at Douglas. "Did you know he was ill?"

"He wasn't just ill," Monty interjected, rubbing his chin. "I've been giving this some thought. He was exhibiting symptoms of a runic infection."

"A what?" I squinted my eyes at him.

Michiko nodded. "It's worse than that, I'm afraid. Much worse."

"How can it be worse? We stopped him and he's down," I said, pointing at Douglas' body. "It's not like he's going to come back, is he?"

"Mage, we have to contain this here." Michiko looked at Monty and then she shoved the conference table out of the way with the push of one hand. "You need to incinerate the body—now."

"What are you taking about? He's not a threat," I said as I entered the conference room, putting my sense of smell at risk.

"If you let the coroner take this body," she said, moving the chairs, "this infection will become an epidemic. I didn't realize he was ill until today when I was attacked."

"The audience yesterday…" Monty said with a nod. "When he went to ask for help, were there other Werewolves present?"

Michiko nodded. "Whatever it was flared today and several Werewolves attacked in a general meeting. They were all present when this Werewolf petitioned for assistance."

"Did they exhibit any flu-like symptoms? Mucus? Shivering?" Monty asked.

"That's why we initially missed it," she said. "By the time we realized what was wrong, they had turned and attacked. Restraints were useless. Three good Werewolves—friends—had to be destroyed today."

"Were those three in contact with anyone else?" I asked.

"She shook her head. "They were in deliberations all day— no outside contact. As far as we can tell, it only affects Werewolves. None of the vampires present seem to be affected."

"Was there a message?" Monty flexed his fingers, and the room grew warmer. "Did they say anything?"

"Yes," she said slowly and turned to Monty.

I looked back and forth between the two of them. "What did they say?"

"They all said the same thing," she said, and stepped back as orbs of fire blossomed in Monty's hands.

"It was a message for me. What was it?" he said, increasing the size of the orbs until I could feel the heat from across the room. "What did they say?"

"*For you*? No," she whispered and looked at Monty again. "Right before they died, they all said one word

—'*Ordaurum*.'"

I could see Monty flex his jaw at the word. "*Ordaurum*. Does that mean anything to you?"

He looked down at his hands and let his hair fall in front of his face, hiding his eyes. The orbs in his palms intensified as he kept his gaze fixed downward.

"No, it doesn't."

My best friend and partner had just lied to me.

THREE

Monty let the orbs float from his hands. For a second, they hung lazily in the air, and Michiko narrowed her eyes as she took a defensive stance and pulled the hairpins from her bun. Her black hair cascaded behind, falling to the middle of her back.

"Chi, what are you doing?" I was alarmed, reading her body language. "No—don't!"

She moved forward a step, when a growling Peaches materialized in front of her.

Michiko froze in place as Peaches' eyes glowed red and runes flowed across his body. She lowered the hairpins and moved back, slowly.

Monty released the orbs and they descended on Douglas' body, reducing it to dust in seconds. He looked up, gave us a tight smile, and moved some hair from his face.

"You thought I was going to attack you?" he said, staring at Michiko as he shook out his hands. "If that time ever comes, vampire, you can trust I won't be using a simple fire spell."

"The Werewolves just snapped," she said, calmly replacing the hairpins in her hair. "They attacked without provocation."

"Monty wouldn't attack you," I drew close to Peaches and rubbed his head. He went from growling to a low rumble. "Right, Monty?"

He looked at me, rolled his eyes and shook his head as he headed back to the kitchen. "I need more tea."

Peaches settled down and winked out of sight. I walked back to the main reception area with Michiko in tow. I could hear Monty pottering around the kitchen.

"Where did it go?" she asked, looking around. "Where did you get that creature?"

"He was a gift from Hades," I said, letting out a breath. "Offspring of Cerberus."

"Hades? As in the god of the Underworld, Hades?"

I nodded. "He felt we were having issues with security and wanted to give us a hand." I worked on the front door finally getting it rehung on its hinges.

"Why doesn't it have three heads? Isn't Cerberus the dog with three heads?"

I peered into the kitchen and gave Monty the 'See? It's not just me' look. He shrugged back at me.

"There were never three heads, at least according to Hades. He just said that to *embellish* the myth, and probably scare people."

"You're serious," she said, looking at Monty and then me. "The god of the dead gave you some kind of hellhound creature, and you both think this is an acceptable gift?"

"We didn't have much of a choice. If we said no he

would have destroyed him."

"That creature—"she started.

"Peaches—his name is Peaches, and he's still a puppy," I corrected. "He doesn't like being called 'creature.'"

"That *creature* needs to be returned or destroyed," she said, looking at me while sitting down on the sofa.

I stared her down. I was the only person I knew who could.

"No," I said, with a shake of my head. "*Peaches* stays until I say otherwise. Now, how do we deal with this infection?"

She remained absolutely still for several seconds without a word. When I was sufficiently creeped-out, she gave me a smile and I stepped back. It was the smile that said 'I can remove your heart and hold it up in front of you while you crumple to the ground, dead.' I never liked that smile.

A cough came from the kitchen and I looked to see Monty give me a quick nod.

"Peaches is part of the household security you advised Simon to rectify on several occasions. He has done exactly as you asked."

"Not *exactly*. But, you're correct. My apologies," she whispered, and gave me a short nod. "If your new *addition* can prevent my phasing into your office, then your security is vastly improved."

She crossed her legs, rested both hands on her knees, and looked at me.

"Do you know what caused the infection?" I asked, sitting across from her. "I'm guessing that's one of the questions you wanted to ask Douglas."

"It's not just the infection the Council is concerned with," she said and turned. "I also must relocate *them*."

She looked at Yama and said something in rapid Japanese. Yama bowed and went into the darkroom. Georgianna followed him in.

"What was that?" I asked. "What did you tell him?"

"I told them both to pack their things. They will be leaving with me," she said as she stood slowly and straightened out her coat.

"Leaving with you? Since when—?" I stopped when I saw Monty give me a look and a quick shake of his head.

"They can't remain here." She gestured languidly with a hand. "This place is no longer safe, even with your... *Peaches*."

"Not safe? Even you couldn't get in without bonding to Peaches."

"Couldn't?" she said and narrowed her eyes. "No, Simon, I *chose* to remain outside your threshold and not destroy your creature."

"How long?" Monty said as he entered the reception area. "How long before the Council sends him?"

"Forty-eight hours, at the most," she said as she pulled out a phone and spoke into it. "Downstairs, ten minutes."

"Why is the Council sending over someone?" I asked.

"Werewolves turned without a moon, which means a high-level mage-spell was cast," Monty said as he watched Yama and Georgianna exit the darkroom. They both bowed and headed out the door. Monty returned the bow. "The Council thinks I'm a threat.

You're here for me."

"I'm here because you're his friend." She gestured in my direction. "This isn't an official visit, this is a courtesy call. They expect you to turn yourself in for a full investigation—by midnight."

I looked at the clock. We had four hours.

"What? I'm sure there are plenty of mages in the city," I said as my anger rose. "They can't assume it's Monty and then expect him to prove his innocence."

"They can and they have. Mage, my suggestion to you is do as they expect."

"There are other mages in the city," Monty whispered while rubbing his chin. "Some just as powerful, if not more powerful than I am. The Hellfire, for instance?"

"You underestimate yourself. There are none of this caliber," she said, walking to the entrance. "None who could work a spell this powerful or complex—except you."

"And if he doesn't turn himself in?"

"The Council is prepared to send Beck to *assist* your mage in cooperating."

"Who the hell is Beck?" I asked. "By 'assist' you mean *terminate*?"

"He's a Negomancer, a sorcerer who deals in the darkest magic. He orchestrates erasures, both magical —and physical," she said after a pause.

"Wait they're going to try and erase Monty?" I stood up, my hand resting on Ebonsoul as I closed the distance to where she stood.

She placed a hand on my cheek and let it rest there for a second.

"Simon, if you get involved in this or try and interfere, Beck *will* kill you."

"Simon—" Monty started.

I held up my hand and he went silent.

"You can stop this," I said, looking at her and placing my hand over hers. "You head the Council. You can stop this order."

She shook her head. "My presence here, warning you, is grounds for my termination—permanently." Her voice was hard as she removed her hand from mine. "You want to stop this? Once you refuse to surrender tonight, find whoever cast the spell, and bring him to the Council. You have until the full moon before they unleash a purge."

"And if we don't find this missing mage?"

She looked at me and stepped past the threshold.

"They will send Beck. You will be seen as an accessory and he *will* kill the both of you," she said and then disappeared.

FOUR

"You're being framed," I said as we moved to the living quarters. "Who wants you stripped of power?"

"Are you serious?" Monty asked as he stepped to a sidewall in our shared office. "You realize I'm over two centuries old. You don't get to my age without making enemies. It's a *long* list."

He placed a hand on the wall opposite our desks and a large section slid back. Inside were our rapid response bags. Two backpacks crammed with everything we needed in case of a quick exit. He pulled them out and placed them on his desk.

I walked over to the wall behind my desk.

"Strongbox?" I asked as I placed my hand on the wall.

"Empty it; I don't want to leave entropy rounds where they can be found," he said while pulling out his phone.

I could hear him speaking with Andrei about getting the Goat ready— our subtle purple Pontiac GTO, which Monty assures me isn't purple but Byzantium— ready as I focused on the wall in front of me. The last time I'd opened this partition, I'd been going to face a deranged god. This situation wasn't much better.

The partition slid back. I pulled out the large, rune-covered strongbox that sat inside. Placing my hand on top of the box made the runes flash orange for a moment before it clicked open. Lifting the lid caused black smoke to waft up into the office and I stifled a cough.

Runes also protected the inside of the box. I picked up the magazines full of entropy rounds for the Grim Whisper and passed most of them to Monty, keeping two for myself.

"Do you know this 'Beck'?" I asked as I slid a magazine into Grim Whisper. I put the spare into the pocket of my coat. "Is he, like, some uber Necromancer?"

Monty shook his head as he adjusted his pack.

"I know of him and none of it is good. Necromancy deals with bringing things back to life.

Negomancy deals with the undoing of things. It's one of the rarest and most obscure disciplines. Sorcerers like Beck have gone so dark that return is impossible. His purpose in the Council is to erase magical abilities among other things."

"Wait, are you saying this Beck has gone over to the 'dark side'? Is he a Sith?"

"Hilarious. You won't feel like joking if you meet him," he said, securing the entropy rounds. "He's dangerous and ruthlessly efficient. The only upside is that Negomancy takes an inordinate amount of power to use. He can only cast for a short time before needing to rest."

"Doesn't sound like much of an upside."

"It's the only one we have. If he can be fatigued, we can stop him before he does any major damage."

"I should be good. It's not like he's going to strip me of magic—I don't have or use any."

He gave me the usual 'Did you really just say that?' stare and sighed.

"Kali *cursed* you alive. What do you think is the basis of that curse—bad intentions?"

"Shit. The curse itself is magic. If he negates it—"

"There goes your immunity to magic not to mention the effect it may have on *you*."

My phone rang as I returned the strongbox and closed the panel.

"Montague and Strong—impossible is nothing. Simon speaking," I answered in my most business-like voice.

"Strong, you need to come see me—now. Bring Tristan."

I recognized the voice. It was Jimmy the Cleaver.

"Jimmy, I'm kind of in the middle of something. Is this urgent?"

"Only if you call setting off every rune in the place urgent."

"We'll be right over," I said and hung up.

"What was that?" Monty asked.

"I think Jimmy has an emergency at the shop. We need to go over there. It may be another infection." I turned and grabbed my pack.

"That—I heard. I meant the way you answered the phone: 'impossible is nothing?'"

"I'm trying out new taglines. I have a few new ones. Did you like that one?"

"No. It was horrendous," he said with an eye-roll and headshake.

We left the living quarters and entered the reception area. Monty made a gesture and secured the door in place.

"Maybe we could start a moving company," I said. "With your ability and my connections—"

"Do you have everything you need?" he said, cutting me off with a glare. "We won't be back for some time."

"Got it," I hoisted the pack on my shoulders, used to traveling light. "What about Peaches?"

As if on cue, he materialized next to me and gave me a low rumble as I scratched his head. Monty looked down at him with a brief nod.

"Somehow I don't think he'll let you out of his sight for any prolonged length of time."

"I have an idea about what we can do with him. Let's go see Jimmy."

Peaches and I stepped out into the hallway and Monty closed the door behind us. We still had a few hours to go before midnight. Neither of us wanted to be here when the time came and the Council decided to bring Monty in by force.

He pressed his hands against the door and then both walls adjacent to the entrance. The door flared white for a split second and returned to normal.

"What was that?"

"That was a temporal fail-safe designed to mark and stop anyone who tries to enter."

"You don't have something that can explode and take them out?"

"Only if you want to have a conversation with Olga about how the second floor of her building is missing."

"On second thought, stopping and marking is good," I said, stepping away from our front door.

We took the stairwell and entered the lobby. Andrei stood by the door and stepped back as Peaches got closer. Outside, I could see the valet had parked the Goat in front of the building entrance.

"*Dosvidaniya*," he said as he opened the door and gave Peaches a wide berth. "Have a good evening."

Monty nodded and stepped outside. I stopped. Part of me wanted to warn Andrei about our impending visitor, but another part of me wanted to torture him with Peaches.

"Andrei," I said, calling him over. He walked over reluctantly. "Someone may come looking for us. Don't get in his way."

He nodded, the look of relief growing with each step back he took away from Peaches. I gave him a reassuring grin as he re-entered the building.

"Why do you torment him?" Monty said as I opened the back door. Peaches jumped in with a bound that strained the Goat's suspension, rocking the car as he settled in the back seat.

Monty walked over to the passenger side and slid in.

"Because it's the little pleasures in life that make it worth living." I jumped into the Goat and started it sitting for a moment and basking in the rumble and purr of the engine.

Monty shook his head, rolling his eyes at my immaturity. "Shall we go?"

Nodding I agreed. "Let's go and see the Cleaver."

FIVE

The Randy Rump had undergone some significant renovations since my last visit. I parked the Goat across the street and got out, Monty and Peaches joining me a second later. I placed my hand on the handle. The engine clanged and the Goat flashed orange, letting me know it was secure. Monty and Peaches joined me a second later.

The Rump stayed open all night, only closing for a few hours in the early morning. It catered to the early evening and nighttime clientele—which was most of the supernatural community. The Rump was also becoming a popular meeting place since the Dark Council declared its neutral status. It had gone from "butcher shop" to "butcher shop, restaurant, and meeting hall" in a few short weeks.

Jimmy had moved the display case and counter to the other side of the room. Tables and chairs filled the remaining floor space. I looked around and saw some of them were filled with patrons who were eating and drinking. Jimmy was behind the counter preparing some sandwiches, and nodded when he saw us come in. He wiped his hands on his apron and came out from behind the counter, motioning for us to follow him.

I counted five vampires stationed around the shop, two by the entrance and the rest spread out among the patrons. The Dark Council always kept members stationed in the neutral locations to ensure they remained neutral.

"The room," Jimmy mouthed and pointed with his head.

"Do you sense an infected Werewolf around here?" I asked Monty as we moved to the back room.

"No," Monty looked around. "But the rune-work makes it difficult to use any magic in here. It's impressive."

"What, dampening runes?"

"Beyond that. Anyone who tries to use any magic or turn in here will be in for a rude surprise."

A few of the patrons gave us looks as we followed Jimmy to the back. Most of them were focused on Monty and Peaches. They could tell he was a powerful magic-user, and Peaches, from what Monty told me, was covered in runes, even though I couldn't see them.

The door and frame to the back room was made of Australian Buloke ironwood and according to Monty,

magically inscribed with runes on every inch of its
surface. It stood ten feet tall and half as wide. Over a
foot thick, opening it was surprisingly easy if you knew
the rune sequence. If you didn't, you'd need the
equivalent of a magical nuke, and that would probably
just scratch the surface. Once closed, it remained
closed. Period.

The backroom of the Rump was considerably
smaller than the front area. It consisted of one large
room with three tables. Two of them, placed along the
north and south walls were long and rectangular. Third
table, in the center was round. Each of them had
seating for seven. Each table was heavy dark oak
inscribed with runes along their surface.

One of the chairs, at the round table, was occupied
by a young woman. She was wearing golden restraints
similar to the silver ones we used against Werewolves.
Her short black hair was peppered with streaks of
silver. Her dark brown leather jacket, jeans were paired
with rugged climbing boots reminding me of a forest
tour guide, about to take us for a hike in the woods.
Her eyes threw me. They were a dark gray with a
highlight of silver that reflected the ambient light—
unlike mine, which were just gray.

"Jimmy," I said, looking around the room, "what's so
urgent? Do you have an infected Werewolf around
here I can't see?"

"Infected Werewolf? Who said anything about
infected? I said she set off every rune in the place," he
pointed at the woman. "She asked for the mage."

Peaches rumbled next to me and fixed his gaze on
the woman at the table.

"Easy, boy," I soothed, scratching him behind the ears.

"Are you Tristan?" she asked, looking at me. "I need to speak to Tristan."

"You're looking for *him*," I answered, hooking a thumb at Monty next to me.

She narrowed her eyes and nodded. "Yes, I see the resemblance."

Monty walked up to the table and sat opposite the girl. I stayed where I was because Peaches was in 'pounce and destroy' mode. He gave off the same vibes when we were talking to Douglas, right before his attack. I unbuttoned my coat and made sure Ebonsoul and Grim Whisper were accessible.

"I need to get back outside," Jimmy said with an apologetic thin-lipped smile. "Will you be okay in here? You should be safe."

I nodded. "I have a favor to ask—later, after we're done in here."

"Whatever you need, let me know. I'm locking the door."

This meant we were on our own. No one was getting through that door, and if things went south, we would have to resolve it on our own. That's what it meant to enter a room of reckoning. No magic, no powers, no special abilities. You go in, settle your differences any way you see fit, and walk out. No judgment. Every neutral location had one.

"I'm Tristan," Monty said, and outstretched a hand. "Pleased to meet you."

She took it and gave it a brief shake, a curious look on her face. His propriety had that effect on people, supernatural or not. I looked at the clock and saw we had an hour and a half before Monty was due at the Council.

"My name is Slif." She removed the restraints from her wrists, absentmindedly massaging her skin where they had been touching. "I have a message for you, from William." She paused for a second. "Please tell your partner over there not to interfere." She glanced briefly at me.

I noticed Monty's hands clench into fists on the table.

"Tell me what?" I asked, stepping closer to Monty concerned by his obvious tension. He held up a hand, stopping me. "Who *is* William?"

"William is *dead*," Monty whispered. "I saw him die."

"No, you saw what he needed you to see, what was necessary at the time."

She stood and placed the restraints in front of her on the table. Her clothes fell away from her body and vanished as she transformed. A few seconds later I stood looking at a something I was told didn't exist.

I was looking at a dragon.

SIX

I moved forward, pulled out Grim Whisper, and took aim. Slif was roughly the size of a small bus, including the tail. Blood-red scales covered her entire body and her gray eyes were now a deep orange. I was looking at a mini-Smaug, minus the wings, and my brain was having a hard time processing it.

"You told me dragons didn't exist, Monty," I said through clenched teeth, trying hard to keep my hand from shaking as I aimed.

"No, I never said that." He was completely calm as he walked to my side, never taking his eyes off Slif. "That was Hades and, technically she's not a dragon."

"That" —I pointed at the large scaled creature in front of us—"isn't a dragon?"

"It's a drake," he said, putting his hand on my wrist and lowering my gun. "And she clearly doesn't want to attack or we would already be fighting for our lives by now."

"What does *it* want? Why is it here?"

Peaches had upgraded from 'pounce and destroy' to 'stalk and destroy' and was closing in on the drake.

"*It* wants you to settle down before someone gets hurt or dead," Slif said and transformed back to human form. Her clothes reappeared and she sat down. "Can you call off your puppy?"

"Peaches, stay," I commanded, and he stopped moving forward.

"Do you have enough to verify authenticity?" she asked, and Monty nodded.

"What does this have to do with William?" Monty's voice was tight.

"Do you know what happens when drake blood is ingested by another species?" she asked, sitting down again and replacing the restraints on her wrists.

Monty sat down and stared hard at Slif. "He didn't."

"No, *he* didn't, but someone else did. Someone close to him."

"Where is he? Where's William?"

"He's gone. Where, I can't say. He tasked me with finding you and then he disappeared. He's very good at not being found."

"Can't or won't?" I said, holstering Grim Whisper and scratching Peaches out of pounce mode.

"She can't," Monty whispered from the table. "Once she takes on her real form, she must speak truth afterwards for a predetermined time."

"For a quarter day, no lie may be uttered by my kind after the transformation. Six of your hours."

"Why did he send you? This is an enormous risk."

"There was no one else to send," she answered. "No one else he could trust."

"An enormous risk to whom?" I asked, looking around. "She's the dragon."

"Drake," corrected Monty, absently. Then, turning back to Slif, his voice hardened. "The message, surely it isn't to mend bridges for the lost decades of absence."

"He wanted to apologize for the deception. He knew it would anger and hurt you. He's sorry he had to do it this way."

"Is that it? An apology for abandoning his family? Tell him not to bother, I'm not interested."

"There's more," she said slowly, spreading out her hands and looking down at the table. "Davros is free."

"Davros…" Monty's face paled. "Impossible."

I was about to ask who Davros was when the earth shook and Peaches disappeared.

SEVEN

"That sounds catastrophic out there," I said, placing my ear to the door. "Who would be insane enough to attack a neutral location?"

Monty backed up and began examining the runes on the door. "Insanity isn't the issue. With the runes out there, who would be powerful enough?"

I gave him a sidelong glance. I checked Grim Whisper and made sure I had a round in the chamber.

"What're you doing?" I asked as I adjusted my thigh sheath. "Tell me you aren't doing what I think you're doing."

"I'm figuring out the sequence to open the door. What did you think I was doing? Admiring the décor?"

"Someone, or more likely *something*, just shook the entire building and you want to go out and do what— say hello?"

He pointed at the runes as he spoke. "There are innocent people out there. I don't relish the thought of being trapped in here while whatever is attacking them figures out a way in here."

"But you won't be able to use your magic out there."

"He will," Slif said and removed the restraints. "He is *Ordaurum*. He is strong enough."

I gave Monty a look as I shifted closer to Slif, against my better sense.

"I don't think so. He's never heard of *Ordaurum*," I said, looking at him.

Monty continued to decipher the door runes. I could

see him stiffen at my words, but he didn't turn around.

"Nonsense," Slif answered and cracked her neck. "He is the ranking *Magus Bellum Ordaurum*. It is the only way I could find him."

"*Magus Bellum Ordaurum*?" I stepped closer to Monty. "My Latin is rusty, but not *that* rusty. "Battle Mage of odor"? Is that what that last part means?"

"We have more important things to focus on at the moment. Step back."

I moved back and he placed his hand on random locations on the door. We waited for a few seconds. Nothing happened.

"Maybe you got the order wrong? Could be you need more bellum and less magus?"

"Bloody hell," he whispered under his breath. "If you persist, I swear I'll scorch you where you stand."

Slif looked at us with a puzzled expression. "Are you two friends?"

"You know, that's a great question. Last time I checked, *friends* don't *lie* to each other."

"I didn't want to get into it in front of your vampire," he replied, still focused on the door. "If she knew I held the honorific she would be forced to try and take me in herself."

"Well, she isn't here. So what does it mean? I'm guessing it's not describing your wonderful scent of magus bellum."

He gave me a quick look and pushed the hair out of his face. "It means battle mage of the Golden Order. I'm the highest ranking battle mage in the Golden Circle."

"So it means you are totally badass? Like, next-level

super-mage badass?"

Slif opened her eyes in surprise. She stifled a giggle behind a series of coughs and looked away.

"*That* is why I didn't want to explain it to you. It means if there is another war, I have to lead the Golden Circle mages to fight and kill—using magic."

"Oh," I said, instantly serious. "That's one hell of a burden. I didn't know, sorry."

"It wasn't cakes and ale last time. I don't plan on going through that again, if I have a say."

"Why would Chi be forced to take you in?"

"*Ordaurum* mages aren't allowed to leave their sects —ever. It's a matter of being battle-ready. If she knew my title she would be forced to attempt to apprehend me and inform the Golden Circle."

"How many of these *Ordaurum* mages does your sect usually have?"

"Five, normally. Only three go into battle at any one time. The remaining two stay back to protect our home —the Sanctuary."

"So what's the issue? They still have four at this Sanctuary place. They don't need you. What about this William? Is he an *Ordaurum* Magus too?"

"Yes. William was" —he looked at Slif—"*is* a battle mage. Together with Davros, a weather mage, we formed the Golden Circle's tribus a TB."

"A what?"

"Three battle mages is a tribus. A TB is a tribus-bellum," he said and waved his hand. "It just means three battle mages."

"What is it with your sect and the Latin? TB sounds like you have a disease."

"Latin was en vogue when the Circle was formed."

"Latin? En vogue? You realize Latin is an old, dead language?"

"The Golden Circle is older. Anyway, the three of us fought in the last war. William was killed, or so I thought. Davros went mad. He had to be negated, restrained, and incarcerated."

He stepped back and placed his hands together. He closed his eyes and whispered something under his breath. I moved farther away from the door as his hands began to glow white. Slif stepped to one side as Monty pressed his hands to the random locations on the door again. My ability to see runes was improving, especially when magic coursed through them. Seeing them in their latent state was still difficult.

This time the runes flared a bright red before going back to normal. The door was open. Monty approached and grabbed the handle. I unsheathed Ebonsoul and held Grim Whisper in my other hand, sensing Slif just behind me.

"Are you sure you want to go out there?"

"I don't see how we have much of a choice."

"What about this William? The one you thought was dead. Why would he send a drag—drake?"

"William…is my older brother," Monty said without turning, and pulled.

EIGHT

An eerie silence filled the room as Monty opened the

large door.

The Randy Rump was a warzone. Chairs and tables lay in different states of destruction. One of the windows near the front door had spider-web cracks running along its entire surface. Parts of the floor appeared to be scorched and a section of the floor near the display case was covered in claw marks several inches deep. At the end of the marks, inside a faintly glowing orange circle, sat Peaches surrounded by runes. The low rumble coming from his direction told me he wasn't pleased, but he didn't move.

Three men closed in on the small bald woman standing in the center of the wreckage. She turned to face us as we stepped into the front room. An intricate tattoo of interwoven designs covered the top of her head and half her face. From the turquoise glow, I could tell the design possessed magical properties. A simple black robe tied at the waist with a white sash covered her slight frame. The sash was interlinked with metal sections which blended into the tail of a white phoenix. The design snaked itself around her waist, up one shoulder and across her chest.

She flashed Monty a brief smile before growing serious. Her piercing black eyes looked past us. A moment later, she averted her gaze to the floor, her face impassive as the men tightened the circle around her.

I could see Jimmy's prone body lying in a corner, still breathing. I took a step toward the woman. Monty grabbed me by the arm and shook his head.

"She hurt Jimmy," I said, pulling against his iron grip. "We have to stop her."

"No," he said, his face grim. "She made sure he was out of the way. Like your creature."

"Those are Dark Council vampires," I whispered and shifted my weight. "She's done."

"Not yet she isn't." He slowly let my arm go. "Don't interfere."

I could feel the heat around him increase, and I noticed that his other hand was flexed. Both his hands were empty as he took a step forward. He bladed his body—turning sideways—making his body smaller and less of a target, and froze in place. Slif moved back, away from him, and I rapidly followed to avoid the instant sauna.

The first vampire launched himself at the bald woman, claws extended. She sidestepped the attack. The claws raked the air next to her face. Simultaneously, as she placed a palm against the attacker's chest, and with one hand she grabbed his other arm. A sudden twist of her waist removed the arm and propelled the vampire through a column.

As she tossed the arm to one side, the second vampire attacked, closing with a blur. He came to a sudden stop as her hand thrust through his chest with her free arm moving horizontally across his lower abdomen. His torso slid away from his legs as the third vampire dashed in with a blade-thrust aimed at her throat.

Tucking her chin she twisted her hand in front of her face, palm in, the edge of her hand both deflected and shattered the blade. The vampire let go of the hilt and raked upward with the opposite hand. She stepped back just enough to cause him to miss, grabbed the arm, and proceeded to flip him over her shoulder. He landed hard enough to crater the floor.

Master Yat's words came back to me: *"The ground is the world's largest fist. Avoid it when you can, use it when you must."*

The vampire, groggy from the impact, didn't have a chance to recover before she slammed a fist down into its head. I felt the impact of the blow from where I stood as the shockwave reverberated throughout the shop. The vampires shifted to dust seconds later. She looked up as she shook their dust from her hands. She had just dispatched three Council vampires in a matter of seconds and wasn't even breathing hard.

Monty hadn't moved. I didn't see any orbs of fire in his hands but I could still feel the heat coming off him.

"Quan," he said, his voice laced with steel, "to what do we owe the pleasure of your company?"

"Tris. She gave him a short nod, which he returned. Her voice could only be described as Elizabeth-Hurley husky. It contained an accent I couldn't place, but it sounded like Monty's part of the world. It was a mix of breathy undertones, good breeding, and an ample dose of menace. "I'm here for the madman you used to call 'friend.'"

I kept Grim Whisper pointed at her. "You killed vampires in neutral territory established by the Dark Council."

"They attacked me, along with that bear," she said, pointing at Jimmy. "I didn't kill *him*."

"Did she just call you Tris?" I asked, glancing sideways at Monty. "Tris?"

"Let it go, Simon," he said with a clenched jaw.

If she could destroy vampires, it meant she was fast, but I doubted she was faster than my trigger finger. But I was wrong. In the space of a blink, she disappeared.

"You must be Simon," she whispered from behind my ear. "You do know entropy rounds only work if you can actually *hit* your target?"

"I make it a point not to miss my targets," I said, doing my best to keep from jumping across the floor while having a heart attack in response to her teleporting. The warmth of her breath caressed my neck and then it was gone. She reappeared again several feet in front of Monty.

"Davros is in this city," she said, and cocked her head to one side with a crooked smile as she looked at his hands. "Do you really want to dance, Tristan? Did you forget last time?"

"I never forget, Quan, you know that."

"Then you recall your searing hand can't cope with my thunderfist and never could. You *will* lose. Besides" —she narrowed her eyes at him—"it looks like your energy is in flux. Are you prepared for your shift?"

Monty didn't answer and remained bladed with his hands flexed. "You don't sense the shift, do you?" she asked, incredulous. "My dear Tris, you *are* in for a surprise."

"Why does the White Phoenix want Davros?" he asked slowly, as if processing her words.

The smile on her face evaporated. "He stole from us. It's in your best interests to turn him over to us—to me."

"It's in your best interests to leave," I said as I holstered Grim Whisper. "The Council will send enforcers."

"Does it look like I adhere to the precepts of your Council?" She turned to me. "What could they possibly enforce against me?"

"Violating the sanctity of neutral territory would be at the top of the list. Followed by attacking and killing Council members, destruction of property, and just being an overall bitch, for starters."

The smile she responded with turned my blood to ice. I realized in that moment I was staring at a killer—a dangerous killer who wielded magic…Shit. I moved my hand closer to my mark.

"What did he steal?" Monty asked quickly. "What did he take from the White Phoenix?"

She kept her eyes on my hands as she answered.

"After he escaped the Circle, he came to us. We accepted him without knowing the full extent of his madness."

"He was negated and incarcerated," Monty whispered to himself. "Escape should have been impossible."

"He wants a purge, Tristan. He has the Phoenix Tail," she said, looking at him. "I have clear orders—recover the Tail and eliminate the target."

"Eliminate?" Monty asked. "Not apprehend?"

"He ingested drake blood. You know the consequences."

Monty shook out his hands and it grew cooler instantly.

"How?" he asked, shooting a quick glance at Slif. "How did he get the Tail?"

"I said he was mad, not unskilled. He's still an

Ordaurum. He overpowered several of the guards and took it before we could stop him."

"And drake blood," Slif said from behind us. "Everything he needs to cast Alder's Permutation."

"And you are?" Quan asked, looking at Slif. "Do I know you?"

"No one of consequence," Slif answered, moving back into the shadows. "I don't believe we've met."

"Not quite everything he needs," Monty said, rubbing his chin. "He needs something more, but it seems he has begun the process with the Werewolves."

"Tristan," Quan said, as the tattoos on her face began to glow, "he's not the person you knew any longer. His mind is gone. The blood will turn him. He's going to start with the Werewolves, but he's not stopping there. You can't reason with him."

"I don't intend to. You'd better leave," he said to Quan. "The Council enforcers will arrive momentarily, and if they see you here, things will escalate."

"They can't stop me," she answered defiantly as she crossed her arms.

"But *I* can," he said with veiled menace. "Do you want to explain to Master Toh how you violated Dark Council neutral territory?"

"You wouldn't dare." She narrowed her eyes at him, the glow increasing in intensity as she stared at Monty.

"Try me."

"I'm going to retrieve the Phoenix Tail. If *anyone* tries to stop me, I will end him."

"If you kill him, you will answer for his death," Monty said, moving the hair from his face. "He is still *Ordaurum*. The Circle will retaliate."

She gave him a brief smile. Something about it made all of the hairs on the back of my neck stand on end. It was a façade of sweetness covering barely contained madness. The little voice I rarely paid attention to was advising me to leave the premises immediately. The words 'unhinged, bat-shit, and psycho' may have been used.

"I only told you because of our history, Tris." She disappeared, only to reappear next to him a split-second later.

"Don't force me to kill you, Quan," he said as the muscles in his jaw flexed.

"I like it when you use force, sweet Tris," she said into his ear and curled a strand of his hair around her finger. "You remember, don't you?"

He pushed her away. "No. Those days are gone. If you touch Davros, I will hunt you down and end *you*."

Her expression darkened. "Your threats are empty against me, Tris," she whispered and kissed his cheek. "If you want your friend to remain breathing, you'd better find him before I do."

"If he gets the third component—" Monty started.

"Then he can complete the Permutation—meaning instant Apocalypse," she said with a wry laugh. She raised a hood, casting her face into darkness . "Either you kill him or I will. The White Phoenix demands his death as the price for stealing the Tail."

She disappeared, leaving echoes of her laughter.

"Bloody hell," he whispered as he pushed hair from his face again. "If they sent her to carry out this sanction, we're in deep shite."

"You have no idea," said a voice from behind us.

It was Ken—the Dark Council's definition of shock and awe.

NINE

"*Kon'nichiwa*, Ken-*sama*," I said, using the honorific. I bowed while simultaneously sheathing Ebonsoul. There was no point in antagonizing him. The little vein throbbing by his temple let me know he was pretty pissed off.

"Cut the shit, Simon," Ken said as he looked around The Randy Rump. "What the hell happened here?"

I slowly looked around the obliterated shop. Ken stood in the center of the destruction. His usual shades of black ensemble were leaning more to the formal side this time. Tonight it was a black shirt with matching tie. Black dress pants and lightly polished shoes—black, of course. All this rested under a black trench coat.

"I'm pretty sure it was an accident," I said, raising my hands in mock surrender. "You know how things can get. We just got here ourselves."

"Do I know how things can get around the two of you? Yes." He knelt down to rub his fingers through the dust on the floor. "Five Council vampires isn't an accident, Strong. Last chance—which mage did this?"

In addition to being an assassin, he was also a master tracker. I didn't know how he knew it was a mage, but he was giving Monty a look I didn't like. He placed a hand on the hilt of the katana across his back. It was rumored to be the sword *kokutan no ken*, the pair to my Ebonsoul. If he drew his weapon, it was going to get bloody fast and people were going to die. I put my hand on Ebonsoul, when a noise grabbed my attention.

"It wasn't them," said a voice from the corner. It was Jimmy, slowly getting to his feet. "We had a guest who set off all of the runes. She vaporized two of your people with a word."

I exhaled the breath I had been holding and slowly let go of Ebonsoul. Quan was more dangerous than I imagined. *Vaporized two vampires with a word?*

Ken looked around, his hand still on the hilt. "Where is this *guest*?"

"She's gone," Jimmy said, brushing off pieces of glass and wood. He stepped over the debris and wreckage and held out a hand. "That was some response time, thanks."

Ken ignored Jimmy's hand and inspected the shop, looking past us to the door of the room of reckoning. I was sure he saw that the runes had been activated.

"Neutral territory is considered sacrosanct," Ken said, releasing the hilt of his sword and looking at me. "Any attack within these walls is punishable by execution. Five Council members are dead, and you're telling me the person—the *mage*—responsible isn't here. Does this walking corpse have a name?"

"Her name is Quan," Monty said, shaking out his hands slowly. "And I suggest you stay away from her."

"Is that a warning or a threat, mage?"

"Whichever keeps you away from her. She's too dangerous."

"Too *dangerous*? Really?" Ken said with a smile and

looked at his watch. "Speaking of dangerous, shouldn't you be turning yourself in to the Council?"

"We think this is connected to the Werewolf infection. Monty can't turn himself in. You said yourself it's a mage. *Another* mage."

"Responsible for this?" He swept his arm around, indicating the shop. "Are you saying there's more than one mage of his caliber loose in the city?"

Monty nodded. "Yes, someone worse than Quan."

Ken slowly shook his head. "It's your funeral. They'll release Beck and he's more the 'lay waste to everything' type. The man has a singular focus that's impressive to see in action."

"I'll deal with Beck," Monty said. "I need you to stay away from Quan."

"She violated Dark Council neutral territory," Ken said, and looking around the shop again before narrowing his eyes at me. "Staying away isn't an option."

I put my hands up. "You're looking at me like I had something to do with this. My destruction is more wholesale."

"True, if this were you, there wouldn't be a shop to stand in."

I nodded and stepped back to regain my balance as Peaches decided that my leg needed immediate protection and proceeded to stand next to me with a low growl.

"Exactly," I said, rubbing him behind the ears. His growl lessened in intensity until it was a barely audible rumble. "Besides, I don't usually do the destroying."

"Death and destruction follow you and your mage

friend here around like a plague."

"I wouldn't say a plague, more like an area of effect."

He turned for the door. "Now you have a hellhound and you're associating with *drakes*, Strong. Michiko won't be pleased about her," he said, looking at Slif.

Slif's face darkened and she stiffened at his words.

"How did you—?"

Ken stopped at the door.

"Did you forget the last *date* you were on? My sister can be somewhat *possessive*. Michiko doesn't share well."

"Does everyone know about this?" I asked. "And this isn't a *date*. She's here to—"

He raised his hand. "Irrelevant. Dragons are dangerous, Strong, even the young ones. Take care of the company you keep," he said without turning around. He lifted his dust-covered fingers to his nose and took a deep breath. "If you'll excuse me, I have a renegade mage to track down and erase. Good luck *dealing* with Beck, mage."

He opened the door and disappeared.

TEN

"Monty, what the hell just happened? Who is your psycho-friend Quan? How are we going to deal with Beck?"

"Quan—is complicated. I thought she was dead. We need to focus on Beck. He won't attack us here. If I were him, I would wait until we left." Monty rubbed his chin and looked around the shop.

"Complicated? Does Roxanne know about her?" I moved around the debris and righted some of the tables. The shop was looking at serious renovations.

"No." He gave me the look that said 'Continue at your own risk.' Never being one to listen to warnings, I did.

"No, she doesn't know? Or no you aren't going to tell her that your deranged psycho lover is visiting?"

"She isn't my lover. We have history, some of it good—most of it violent. She's always been unstable. It's part of what made her a fearsome ally." He brushed the dust off his sleeves and moved to inspect the runes etched into columns.

"You know, I didn't get the ally vibe. It was closer to an 'I will remove parts of you' vibe."

"She isn't the priority. We have to figure out how she got around the runes in here," he said, stepping away from the column he moved over to the faded containment circle she'd used to hold Peaches.

I followed him. "Runes? Didn't you hear Ken? This Beck sounds like a nightmare to deal with."

"He is. Beck is one of the only practicing Negomancers left in this hemisphere. His skill and abilities are formidable."

He crouched down and examined the claw marks that ended at the outer edge of the circle.

"Well, that puts my mind at ease, thanks. We're staying here because you want to do what—catch up for old times' sake?"

"We're staying because we need information. Besides, this is still neutral territory. Even Beck would hesitate to attack here. He may be unstable, but he follows the rules."

"You never said anything about him being unstable," I said. "What is it with you mages? Wait—did you say *hesitate*?"

Monty gave me a short nod. "Quite unstable, actually. Now, let's use the time we have. What do you see, Simon? Tell me. Recreate it."

I knew what he was doing. He was engaging my brain to take my mind off our impending confrontation with Beck.

"We should just leave. We can discuss it over dinner at Roselli's," I said, looking at the door nervously. "You know, where it's less likely a deranged mage will attack us?"

"It doesn't matter where we are, really. Though we have a better chance facing him here than Roselli's."

I stepped over to the entrance of The Randy Rump and closed my eyes. I took a deep breath and focused. I had possessed this skill even before Kali decided to reach out, curse me, and turn my life upside down and inside out. It's what made me one of the best detectives in the city.

"She came in about ten minutes after we did," I looked down at the dust piles of the two vampires she vaporized first. They rotated in shifts around the shop and I noticed two of the remaining three that attacked her were at the door when we walked in. "The guards must have just switched locations. She took these two down fast and all hell broke loose."

"I agree, though she must have held a considerable amount of energy to undo two vampires while in here," Monty said as he approached my side and examined the runes on the doorframe.

"That must have been the tremor we felt. Peaches came out, but she froze him in that circle over there," I said, pointing at the claw marks that ended in a faintly glowing runic circle. "Jimmy must have tried something and she introduced him to the glass."

Jimmy nodded. "Couldn't transform but I tried to stop her and she just sent me flying. You're good, Simon."

"Just something I picked up over the years," I said and looked at Monty. "Now would be a good time to go."

Monty walked back to the circle that had kept Peaches in place. He closed his eyes and ran a hand over the surface of the floor. He then stepped over to the columns in the shop and examined the runes on each of them again. The runes in the shop were designed to negate any use of magic within the space. Their placement was strategic to create a self-sustaining field of negation.

"How did she manage to use her ability without setting the runes off?" he whispered more to himself than to us. "James, what did you see?"

"Right after you all arrived and went into the room, in she walks. Quiet, and smelling of magic."

"Smelling of magic?" I asked. "What kind of scent?"

"It's hard to describe. She smelled like cinnamon mixed with something else. I didn't give it much thought because of the runes and we're on neutral ground."

"Just another mage, coming in for a drink," I said. "You get a lot of mages in here?"

He nodded. "They don't come in often, but I have a few regulars, mostly low level. Not like him," he said, pointing at Monty with his chin.

"Trust me, there isn't another one like him anywhere on the planet, thankfully."

Monty gave me a look and shook his head.

"What happened after she came in? Did she sit?" Monty asked.

"I asked her if she wanted a seat and she said no. Then she stood over there." Jimmy pointed to an area near the entrance in between the piles of vampire dust. "She said something in a language I didn't understand. All the runes went off with a shockwave, and the two Council vampires next to her turned to dust. I figured we were under attack and jumped at her. She sent me over her shoulder into the window."

"She bypassed the failsafes and undid the vampires in one stroke," Monty said, following Jimmy's arm with his eyes. "Show me exactly where she stood."

Jimmy came over and pointed to the space near the door. Monty went over and stood there. His face transformed from calm to surprise.

"Of course," he said and moved his hands in a gesture I recognized. It meant we had just run out of time. "James, is there another exit we can use? Perhaps through the room?"

Monty had just thrown up a shield. I checked the mala Karma had given me and made sure I had access to it. The mark on my left hand throbbed but I didn't sense her. This was something else.

Jimmy nodded. "In the back of the room, there's one. It's runed to prevent anyone from getting in that way."

I looked at Monty and he shot me a quick glance. It told me everything I needed to know.

"Shit, everyone to the room. Now!" I yelled. "He's coming, isn't he? It's Beck?"

Monty, his face grim, nodded.

We started running to the room of reckoning, when the front of The Randy Rump exploded.

ELEVEN

Monty's shield contained the explosion. Glass, wood, and concrete remained frozen in mid-air. The entire façade, along with some of the sidewalk, had been obliterated and was headed in our direction. Now Ken would definitely think we were involved. And to be honest, it *was* more our style.

"What happened to 'even Beck would hesitate to attack here'?" I said as I pushed pieces of broken tables and glass away. "Doesn't look like he hesitated much."

"We need to get them into the room and away from him," Monty said and made another gesture. I saw the shield shimmer and grow opaque.

Peaches padded over to me and gave a short snuffle. Other than the dust covering his body, I saw no damage. I was beginning to think he was indestructible. I couldn't see outside but I knew Beck was out there. There was an empty presence tugging at the fringes of my consciousness.

"I can feel him. I mean, not feel him. He feels like an empty hole," I said as I stood unsteadily, rubbing Peaches.

"It's what he is and does." Monty shook off some of the dust. "Get to the room. I'll slow him down."

"No," I said as my phone rang. "Jimmy, take Slif and Peaches and get in the room. Make sure the door is locked."

I connected the call as Jimmy ran for the back room with Slif and a reluctant Peaches in tow.

"Simon, what are you doing?" Monty started as I raised a finger, indicating the phone.

"Strong," Ramirez's strained voice came over the line. "I have a situation that requires your presence."

"I was just about to say the same thing, Angel, or is that 'Director Ramirez' now?" I said, putting the call on speakerphone. "Now that you're all important."

"You can call me *Director* Ramirez, comedian. Is Tristan there?"

"I am," Monty said and stepped behind a column, prompting me to do the same. "Our attention is currently engaged in a pressing matter at the moment."

"Where are you?" Ramirez asked. "I'm at The Den. You know it?"

"58th and 11th. The exclusive Werewolf club. Members-only upscale place; yes, I know it," I said, making sure I stayed behind the column.

"How soon can you get here?"

"Can't say. This situation is fluid at best," Monty answered and looked around the column.

"I have a rabid Werewolf on the loose. I lost one

man and I have another three injured. Restraints were as effective as toilet paper on this guy."

"Sounds like you have a handle on the situation," I said. "We're currently dealing with a Negomancer who works for the Dark Council—scary bad guy."

"A what? Never mind, yours sounds worse. Do you need backup?"

"Yes," I said, trying to get a glimpse of Beck. "Backup would be *shaynetastic*."

"No," Monty said, shaking his head. "Backup will get someone killed."

"What's your location?" Ramirez asked again. "I can send over a squad with my second-in-command, Cassandra. She can handle herself."

"We're at The Randy Rump," I said, instantly regretting it.

"You're where? Something you want to share?" Ramirez chuckled.

"It's a meat shop. I didn't name it."

"I bet it is. Listen, your life, your choices. No judging here. Send me the location of your randy rump," he said, stifling another laugh.

"This is a bad time." Monty gestured with his hand. He signaled to me, and I drew Grim Whisper.

"And her name is Cassandra, not Cass or Cassie, and don't even try Sandra or she just might make you a eunuch."

"She sounds pleasant," I said. "Tell her not to engage until we've neutralized the threat, Ramirez, or she gets dead. I'm serious, this guy is dangerous. I still think this is a bad idea."

"I'm not asking, Simon. She and her squad will form

an outer perimeter and monitor from there."

Then it clicked. He was trying to get rid of her.

"So how much of a pain in the ass is she?"

"Enough that I need to get her out of this situation before she gets herself killed, and my ass fired. She's the daughter of one of the brass. Perimeter duty is perfect."

I moved to another column in time to see a blob of dark energy smash into Monty's shield and disintegrate it.

"Tell her to stay two blocks away, no closer. Got to go," I said and hung up.

Monty began inscribing runes into the floor behind the column. "What the bloody hell is *shaynetastic*?"

"Your shield is down and you're worried about *shaynetastic*?" I said, making my way to the display case.

"I'm aware of the status of the shield I created," he said, tracing more runes into the floor and moving to another column.

"It means beyond awesome. Like it? Feel free to use it. Probably sounds better when you say it."

"It's not even English."

"It's American and it's hot right now," I grabbed a bottle of iced coffee from the display case there's always time for coffee. "I hear a wizard in St. Louis started it. It's the newest thing."

"That just means it's gibberish," he said and moved to another column, repeating his rune tracing. "Wizards."

"Not gibberish—slang. Otherwise known as the evolution of language."

"More like an abomination of the language—

otherwise known as English," he said as he finished a rune. He ran behind the display case and made another gesture. I saw a shimmering wall go up that connected the runes he had traced.

"Won't he just throw another glob of the black energy?"

"I'm counting on it," he said and covered us in another shield.

TWELVE

"Tristan Montague, by the authority of the Dark Council, I order you to surrender yourself for incarceration until such time that the Council deems you innocent or you undergo erasure," Beck yelled from outside the Rump.

"Sod off, Beck!" Monty answered from behind the display.

Beck grunted. "Eloquent as usual, Tristan. Why not just give yourself up and make this easier for the both of us?"

I heard the crunching of glass and knew he was getting closer.

"He sounds like a lot of fun," I said as I moved away from the approaching footsteps.

"If by fun you mean an uptight toff, then yes, he is incredibly fun." Monty moved down to the other end of the display case, away from Beck. "Brace yourself. I'm going to prod him a bit."

The footsteps stopped inside the Rump. I peeked

over the display case to catch a glimpse of Beck. He was an average-sized man of medium build. Surprisingly he didn't wear a trench coat, just a brown jacket and a matching tie. His black hair was cut low but not too close. He looked normal except for his hands being covered in black energy—oh, and the tears. He was crying black tears.

"Either he's wearing the world's cheapest mascara or he's leaking black energy from his eyes," I said, ducking back behind the display. "Both situations are disturbing."

"It's an effect of the Negomancy," Monty said, tracing a rune in the floor. "He has to bleed off the energy he's negating or it will kill him."

"Tristan, your insignificant wall isn't going to stop me," Beck moved around the perimeter of the runic wall Monty set up, gathering black energy in his hands as he paced. "This is pointless."

"Much like your position within the Council? When was the last time you had a real mission?"

I saw Beck clench his jaw and the black energy around his hands increased.

"Monty," I whispered, crouching next to him, "this doesn't sound like a good idea. How about we just blast him into next week and run for it?"

"He would just absorb the energy. In order to fight Negomancy with magic, you would need three to four mages attacking at once to overwhelm him. Even then I don't know if it would be enough."

"How about one detective with many bullets?" I pointed at Grim Whisper.

"Kinetic energy is still energy. What good are

entropy rounds if the bullets fall to the floor as they leave the barrel? This is why I need him to attack. And put that away before someone gets shot."

I holstered Grim Whisper and glanced through the display case to see Beck getting closer.

"Stop wasting time, Tristan," Beck said, stepping into fighting stance and looking around. "If you're innocent we can clear this up; and if not, justice will be swift."

"Justice?" I could hear the anger rise in Monty's voice. Never a good sign. Right now, the room of reckoning was looking like a good idea, but I was sure Jimmy had locked the door. "I seem to recall your idea of 'justice' entailed destroying those less powerful than you."

"I did what I had to do, Tristan. We all did— including you."

Beck was looking in our direction. He was using the conversation to pinpoint our position in the shop.

"Bollocks. You went above and beyond," Monty answered. "You killed and erased countless innocents."

A cruel smile crossed Beck's face as he gave a mock bow.

"What can I say? I take pleasure in my work. Unlike you, I take pride in my abilities. That's the difference between us, Tristan. I embrace who and what I am. You live in denial."

"Actually it's called the Moscow," I countered. "Great views of the Hudson."

"Get ready," Monty whispered to me. He stood and stepped out from behind the display case and the shield. "You are a petty thug who is either too ignorant or too deluded to understand that the Council is just keeping you around to suit their purpose. You're no better than a rabid dog kept on a short leash that is released when they want a spurious problem *solved*."

Beck's face darkened and he released both blobs of black energy at Monty. They smashed into the wall, destroying it. Monty rushed forward and closed the distance. The runes on the floor flared to life, shooting tethers of black energy at Beck.

"These runes…" Beck started as he struggled against the tethers and tried to step back, "how could you know the backlash?"

"You have no idea what I know," Monty said and gesturing with one hand while touching the ground with the other.

The tethers wrapped themselves tighter around Beck and slammed him to the ground. He was slowly being encased by the black energy as it dragged him out to the street.

"No mage knows that spell," Beck said and narrowed his eyes. "Unless you've gone dark. Is that it, Tristan? You've gone dark, haven't you? That would explain your strange energy signature."

"Bloody hell, Beck," Monty muttered and stood, pushing a strand of hair from his face. "You never did know when to shut it. If I had gone dark, I wouldn't have used the backlash. I'd have used something nastier, like a void, and be done with you."

Beck's eyes widened slightly as he clenched his jaw. "You wouldn't dare. The Golden Circle prohibits use of any void spell in a populated location. You would have more than me to worry about."

Monty stepped over to him and crouched down.
The black energy had reached Beck's neck and was
creeping upward. His entire body was immobilized,
preventing any kind of motion. Beck grunted and
strained against the cocoon.

"All you ever cared about were the rules. You came
here, threatened me with erasure, and expected—what?
A cheery welcome?"

Monty stood and looked down. He dusted off his
sleeves and walked back into the Rump.

"Rules, Tristan. That was always your problem.
Without them, we are nothing but savages with power.
Rules make the difference between us and them."

Monty clenched his fists and stopped midstride.
"The next time I see you, I won't be so courteous."

"Nor will I," Beck managed before the energy
covered his face and silenced him.

Monty walked quickly past me and headed to the
room of reckoning. He began to touch parts of the
door. I saw the runes flare, but the door didn't open. I
looked back at Beck's prone form. He was moving so I
guessed he was still alive.

"Is that thing going to kill him?"

Monty gave me a withering glare. "If I wanted him
dead, there are less complicated ways of removing
him," He looked back at the encased Beck. "It's energy.
He won't suffocate, but he *will* break free. When he
does we need to be elsewhere."

I pointed to what used to be the front of The Randy
Rump. "Why don't we just walk out that way?"

Monty grabbed a green bottle of overpriced water
from the top of the display case and tossed it outside.

It sailed lazily through the air and landed ten feet behind Beck, rolling as it hit the ground. I was about to speak when Monty held up his hand.

"Give it a second."

A bright flash blinded me. When I could see again, the bottle was gone—along with a sizable chunk of the street.

"Well, shit. That is all kinds of wrong," I said, looking at the charred crater where the bottle landed.

"It's a particular type of Negomancy. Magical mines that convert latent energy into thermal. Beck favors this kind of deception. I prefer not wasting time or valuable energy unraveling them. Better if we find another way out."

He went back to work on the door runes, when I heard the engine.

"Monty, how far do you think mines extend from the front of the shop?" I moved to the entrance and looked up the street.

"No, you can't jump over them. Wait—why?"

I pointed up the street. In the distance, I saw the blue flashing lights of the NYTF.

"We may have company."

"Bloody hell," he said as he ran outside gesturing at the same time. Each hand moved in a different intricate sequence. It reminded me of the time I watched a virtuoso play Rachmaninoff.

The cop car shuddered sideways and came to a sudden stop. A gust of air rushed down the street toward it and shoved it back. The tires left skid marks as they resisted the backward motion and twisted off the axles. I saw the ground around him glow red. I swore Beck laughed right before the world erupted.

THIRTEEN

The shockwave punched me in the chest and flung me back, bouncing me off the display case. I staggered to my feet and shuffled to the front of the shop. I shook the glass out of my hair and looked outside, expecting to see the worst.

Monty had surprised me with his magical ability many times. I didn't really know how powerful he was in the scale of magical beings. Was he weaker than a god but stronger than an ogre? There was no real way to tell from what I'd seen. We'd run from ogres and faced gods so it could get a bit confusing at times. The one thing I was always certain about when it came to him was that I was damn glad he's on my side.

He stood in the middle of a wide, burned out trench. His suit smoldered as he slowly climbed out. Smoke wafted around him, and the air was thick with the smell of molten asphalt. Beck's body was still encased in black energy, but his head was now free.

"That looked painful, Tristan," he jeered. "A shame you only detonated about half of them. No matter, my work is done and you—"

His words were cutoff as Monty gestured and the energy covered his face again.

"Shut it," Monty whispered as he headed for the NYTF cruiser. I stepped close to him, careful to follow his footsteps and not set off any other mines.

"You okay?" I kept my gaze down, trying to make out the runes before I stepped on them. My ability to see them had improved. Monty said it had something to do with holding the essences of the ten sorcerers Chaos had placed in me. Having them inside me was waking up some dormant skill.

"Do I look okay?" he answered testily, flexing his fingers as we approached the cruiser.

"Well, you look well done, like a good skirt steak. The suit, though, trashed."

He gave me a look and shook his head. I rested my hand on Grim Whisper once we got to the cruiser. I knew Ramirez was sending over his lieutenant, but it was clear she didn't follow instructions. A woman sat inside the car and looked at Monty. She stepped out and stood with her legs slightly apart. She was visibly shaken but was doing a good job of keeping it under control.

The weight of her body rested on the balls of her feet and I could see she had some training. She was about five-and-a-half feet tall with short brown hair. Her eyes held intelligence and she clearly wore the 'I will beat you with your own arms if you cross me' vibe. To her credit, she kept her weapon holstered.

"What did you think you were doing?" Monty asked, looking around. "Where is the rest of your team? Didn't Ramirez mention a squad?"

I nodded. "Cassandra?" I held out my hand. She took it and gave me a firm shake. "You were supposed to set up a perimeter. You nearly drove into permanent early retirement."

"Lieutenant Cassandra," she replied, looking at the

damage behind us. "Ramirez told me to pick you up. From what I saw, a perimeter wasn't going to help. I'm here to pick you up—now."

"No. I refuse," Monty said and headed back to the Rump. "I already deal with you all the time, Simon. I refuse to deal with the female version of you. Handle this and get her away from here before she detonates herself."

He walked away while still muttering to himself.

"What's his damage?" she asked, looking at Monty's retreating back. "We have a situation uptown that needs both of you."

"He's old and cranky and he just set off some magical mines to make sure *you* didn't. Tends to put him in a foul mood."

She gave a short nod and checked her weapons. I realized it was her method of dealing with the stress of facing the unknown.

The New York Task Force or NYTF, was a quasi-military police force created to deal with any supernatural event occurring in New York City. They dealt with all the strange, unexplained events that occurred in the city. Each NYTF agent underwent extensive psych training and evaluations, but most of them lost it from prolonged exposure to the supernatural. The churn rate was over ten percent. A few of them would go full psychotic break and get a room at Haven Medical for an extended vacation.

The NYTF wasn't for the timid. It meant she was tough. To make lieutenant meant she was intelligent and skilled, or connected. Still didn't explain why she would choose the NYTF.

"What situation? We kind of have our hands full here." I turned to follow Monty. "And you don't have a vehicle."

"Ramirez is going to kill me for this. He's really touchy about the company vehicles," she said, looking at the cruiser. "What the hell did he do anyway?"

"Ramirez is always touchy, and you don't really want to know, do you? You can hitch a ride with us," I pointed to the Goat parked down the street.

"Not really, no," she said as she caught up with me. "I can brief you on the way. Ramirez just said to get your asses uptown now."

I pulled out my phone and dialed Ramirez. He picked up on the third ring. He was picking up bad habits.

"Tell me you're on your way, Simon." I heard gunfire in the background. "Because if you're not, I have nothing to say to you."

"Your lieutenant is here. What happened to the squad? We have a psycho—"

"Exactly, you have *one* psycho. I'm dealing with three Werewolves now who want to have a shredding party. Get in the car and get your asses here now!" he yelled and hung up.

Cassandra looked at me with a slight smile across her lips and the 'I told you so' face. I hated that look.

"We need to secure this area before we rush uptown, or else this place is going to be messy," I said, walking around the trench and heading into the Rump.

She stood at the edge of the trench and stared at the devastation. "Did you say it was 'going to be' messy?" she asked.

"You'd better wait over there," I said pointing to an area I thought was safe. "Some of the mines might still be live. Wouldn't want to see you scattered all over the place."

She looked down sharply and took a few steps back.

"I think I'll wait here," she said, still looking at the damage around her. "Ramirez said you guys were a demolition team. I thought he was kidding."

I smiled as I turned to enter the Rump. I looked around for Beck, but his body was gone. I drew Grim Whisper and made my way inside. The door to the room of reckoning was open, but I didn't see anyone.

"Monty?" I called out. "Where are you?"

"In here." I heard his voice come from the room. "We have a situation."

I ran into the room and saw Jimmy lying on the floor. He shivered uncontrollably. Sweat covered his face and he stared blankly up at the ceiling. Slif and Peaches stood off to one side. Peaches walked up, gave me a sniff, and bumped into my leg, almost knocking me down.

"I'm good, boy," I said, rubbing his ears and looking at Monty. "What happened? Where's Beck?"

"A variation of what occurred to Mr. Bishop earlier today. This is an effect of Alder's Permutation," Monty said and closed the door behind me. "We need to get him to Haven before he transforms. Beck was gone when I returned. I'm sure we'll run into him again."

"We need to get uptown. Ramirez is dealing with three Werewolves out of control and it doesn't sound good. It's why we only got Cassandra."

"If we remove James from this room, he will turn

and we will be dealing with a crazed bear," Monty said, rubbing his chin. "But there may be a way."

"Whatever it is we need to do, do it fast. Ramirez sounded pissed."

"I need you to get the car and bring it to the front as close as possible to the entrance," Monty said and began tracing a rune on Jimmy's chest.

"What about the mines? I'm not in the mood to explode. I thought you said if we take him out he turns?" I looked down at the shivering sweaty form.

Monty ran a hand through his hair. Sweat covered his brow and some of the hair stuck to his forehead. "The mines are disabled. The runes on the car should prevent the transformation," he said as he finished the tracing. "They should keep him in stasis long enough for us to get to Haven and Roxanne."

"Hey, you okay? I mean, really? I've never seen you break out in a sweat."

He waved away my words. "I've been in the middle of an explosion, fighting a Negomancer, and deciphering the runes on this door. I haven't eaten, and the neutralizing runes in this place are working overtime to thwart my magic-use. Pardon me for some exhaustion."

I raised my hands in surrender and headed to the door. "Just asking. No need to tear my head off. Can you open this?" I gestured at the door.

He came over, touched several runes in sequence, and the heavy wooden door whispered open.

"I apologize," he said after a pause. "It would appear my resources are being taxed more than I imagined. I really should get some food."

"Butcher shop," I said, looking around once he opened the door. "Not really your kind of menu. Don't you have your veggie mage power bars in the car?"

He nodded. "I'll grab one on the way uptown," he said, leaning against the door. "We need to find Davros before Quan does. If she gets to him first, things will escalate out of control."

"What about Beck and the Council?" I asked as I patted my jacket, looking for the keys to the Goat. "He seems dangerous."

"He is," Monty handed me his keys when my search turned up empty. "We find and stop Davros, they'll call off Beck. Besides, the idea of Quan roaming the streets of New York City is unsettling."

"We're going to have to take Cassandra with us. Your airbrake trashed her car."

"If she had followed instructions, it wouldn't be an issue," he said and took off his ruined jacket. "She's worse than you are."

"Not possible," I stepped outside the room and he closed the door behind me as I stood in the middle of the obliterated shop. Renovation wasn't an option anymore. Tearing it all down and starting from scratch was the only hope for the Rump now. The Dark Council would cover the costs. All neutral locations were covered with destruction insurance for situations like this. Maybe they should call it mage insurance.

I ran around the trench and across the street to the Goat, placing my hand on the handle and unlocking it. An orange wave of light danced over the surface and the door unlocked. The engine did its 'hammer on anvil' clanging and I jumped in and started it. I paused for a second to enjoy the rumbling and backed it up to the Rump.

Monty and Slif came out, carrying Jimmy. I got out to assist as we put him in the back seat. I saw a red glow dance over the car as we got him settled.

"What was that?" I asked warily, looking at the Goat in case it decided this was a good time to detonate.

"The runes inscribed in the vehicle attune to the supernatural," Monty said, strapping a seatbelt around Jimmy's large torso. "It was recognizing James—or rather the werebear he is. In this case, the car will act like a restraint and prevent his turning. I hope."

"As long as it doesn't have any lethal fail-safes, I'm good. Wait—what do you mean you hope?"

"It's not always an exact science. We're dealing with an old, powerful, and dangerous spell. I'm pretty sure it will work." He signaled to Cassandra as he opened the other door for her.

Peaches bounded in next to her and went into auto-rumble mode. Cassandra gave him a sideways glance and slid a little closer to Jimmy.

"Is this your—? I want to say dog, but I'm not sure that applies. More importantly—does he bite?" She opened her jacket to allow access to her gun.

I slid into the driver's side and rested my hands on the wheel. "Yes and yes. He's a good dog, just don't violate his personal space and you'll be okay."

"Violate *his* space? He's taking up half the seat."

"He's being generous. He usually gets the *entire* back seat." I gave him a look. "Move over, and don't eat her."

He shuffled closer to the door with a low growl and

gave me a disappointed look before he stuck his head
out of the window and ignored me. Cassandra let her
hand rest on her holster and kept her eyes locked on
Peaches. I guessed she wasn't a dog person.

Monty stood next to Slif just outside the Goat.

"Do you have anything else to tell me?" he asked,
looking at her. "I'm afraid we can't offer you a ride. I
didn't figure meeting a drake when the runes were
created. Your presence inside the vehicle would have—
unpleasant consequences."

She shook her head. "I understand. I must get back
anyway." She stepped back.

"Can you tell me anything about his whereabouts?"
Monty asked. "Anything that can point me to William?"

"I'm sorry. He's hidden from my sight. There is
another of your kind, a mage—quite powerful—with
the blood of dragons flowing within. I can sense *him*."

"Davros," Monty said, flexing his hands. "Where?"

She closed her eyes for a few seconds, and then
pointed. She was pointing north.

"How far?" I asked, craning my neck to look in the
direction she indicated.

"About two or three miles. You must cross a river
and then find the island of siblings. He will be there."

"Thank you." Monty gave her a slight bow.

"Drake blood is poison to you. It can bestow great
power, but not without a cost. No human can drink of
it and remain sane." She removed the restraints around
her wrists.

"The problem is Davros hasn't been sane for some
time," Monty replied, giving her room. "Dragon blood
wouldn't make matters worse."

"Find him and stop him before my kind become involved," she said as a golden light covered her and she transformed into her dragon form. She raced across the street and leaped into the air, disappearing into the night sky.

"I thought dragons couldn't fly without wings?" I said as I tried to track her. "What did she mean before her kind gets involved? Do we want them involved?"

"Dragons don't get involved in human affairs. Even during the war they chose to go into hiding rather than pick a side," he said as he got in the Goat. "This time it may be different."

"Why is this different? I can't think of a scenario where adding dragons makes it better. Well…unless you're being chased by angry Werewolves—then adding a dragon to chomp on the Werewolves would work," I said as I handed him one of his mage power bars. He took it with a nod.

"Adding dragons to the mix here is the worst-case scenario, since they don't compromise or negotiate, just reduce everything to ashes. Literally and figuratively," he said before taking a bite of his bar. "More importantly, I don't trust them. Everything they say is open to interpretation and they operate by their agenda —always."

"Are you saying she lied about the location?" Why would she?"

"She's a drake. That would be reason enough."

"We need to do some recon before following up on her intel, then. Ramirez might know what she was talking about. This Davros is either on Randalls or on Rikers Island. I've never heard of an island of siblings.

You think it's a trap?"

"I think we don't go rushing there without more information. Let's deal with the immediate concern," he said and looked in the back seat at Jimmy and Cassandra. "We need to get to Haven."

FOURTEEN

Haven Medical was remodeled after an ogre decided to redecorate the building by destroying everything in its path. Most of it was cosmetic, except for the runic defenses. Roxanne DeMarco, the director of the facility —and a sorceress—had reinforced the runes around the property and on every floor after our last 'visit' to Haven resulted in half the facility being demolished.

Monty had called ahead and she met us in the ambulance bay, which led to the hospital's emergency department. A pair of large men pushed a gurney next to the car and unloaded a shaking and trembling Jimmy while Roxanne supervised. She was a tall, slim brunette with deep green eyes you could get lost in. There was a small scar across her forehead, courtesy of the ogre we fought.

Showing my age, I called out her name in my best rendition of Sting from the song by The Police. She winced and shook her head. "Truly, that never gets old, Simon. I could cast a vocal cord removal spell and help you with that affliction you have?"

"No, thank you. Monty would miss out on my amazing impromptu concerts," I said after hitting a particularly high note, which caused Peaches to whine. He was clearly tone-deaf.

"Oh yes, what ever would I do without your ear-splitting, migraine-inducing concerts?" Monty said as he got out of the Goat and walked over to Roxanne. He gave her a short nod, which she returned. This was what passed for passion between them, which I didn't point out because he was being extra cranky and I didn't want to be target-practice.

Besides, I wasn't in much of a position to judge; at least Roxanne didn't go around ripping people's throats out, unlike a certain vampire I knew. I shook my head and looked into the back of the Goat. Cassandra held up her wrist and pointed to it. We were running short on time.

I nodded in response and held up one hand with splayed fingers indicating five minutes. She gave me a short nod and went back to staring at the oblivious Peaches. He had sprawled to take up more space once Jimmy was removed, forcing Cassandra to the other side of the seat.

"I have to say, it's refreshing and a little surprising you arrived here without some disaster chasing you," Roxanne said, looking at me.

"Hey, I don't do mobile disasters. That would be him," I gestured to Monty with a shake of my head. She turned to him and rested a hand on his arm.

"Tristan, we need to keep the patient contained in runic stasis." She looked down at the clipboard she held. "Can you ensure the nurses get it right? Last thing I need is a crazed werebear running amok through the halls."

"How many layers of redundancy does your stasis have now?" he replied. "Three layers wasn't enough last time."

"After the ogre"—she gave him a tight smile and self-consciously touched her scar—"we increased it to ten layers."

Monty raised an eyebrow in surprise. "I've never seen more than eight layers. Ten is impressive." He turned toward the commotion. "I'll be back shortly."

"Thank you, Tristan," she said, squeezing his arm gently causing him to pause and blush. He nodded and took off after the two men who were pushing Jimmy into the facility.

"Doesn't he ever notice when you're trying to get rid of him?" I asked her as we stepped away from the Goat.

"Sometimes even the most perceptive can be blinded by emotion." She looked past me and into the Goat. "Who's your friend? Does your vampire know you are dating? Your passenger seems to be in a state of shock. Or is that fear?"

"It's Peaches, and he has that effect on everyone who meets him in close quarters. She's *not* my friend. She's NYTF and works with Ramirez. We aren't dating," I said, throwing a hand in the air. "Is there anyone in this city who hasn't heard about that night?"

A short laugh escaped Roxanne and then she quickly grew serious. She moved away a few more feet from the Goat and then made a gesture. I recognized it from sitting with Monty at Roselli's. The sounds around us immediately muffled. She had just cast a sphere of silence.

"Did Monty teach you the mute spell too?" I asked after a few seconds of surprise. My voice bounced around a few times. The echoes slid into each other and then settled into a normal pattern.

"Mute spell? This evocation of silence belongs to sorcerers. Subtlety isn't what mages are known for, if you haven't noticed."

"I've noticed and so have many of the buildings in the city. So you taught it to him?"

She nodded. "Something's wrong with Tristan," she said, urgency lacing her words. "His energy signature is all over the place. It's almost as if he's gone—that can't be right."

"Gone where?"

"Not where, what," She gestured again and a small orb the size of a grapefruit materialized in her hand. It hung there and bobbed slowly as it rotated appearing as a deep indigo surrounded by a black circle of energy. "This is Tristan, or rather a representation of his energy signature—his magic."

"Is that black circle getting bigger? That can't be good."

"That circle is only present when a magic-user has gone dark. But it doesn't make sense here. It should be invading the center, taking it over. Not encasing it."

"What are you saying?"

She turned the orb in her hand. "Only the strongest mages have this blue energy signature. The only color above it is gold and I have never encountered that color."

It looked mostly solid, but some parts were becoming transparent. It flashed and I saw it grow smaller. The black circle increased to take up the space.

"The blue is getting smaller." I noticed with a hint of panic in my voice.

"Yes. If it continues, Tristan will lose his ability to control his magic," she said, her voice grim. She closed her hand and the orb evaporated.

"He'll lose his magic?" I was alarmed at the idea of Monty without his magic. I didn't know what happened to a mage when they were erased, but I was positive it was bad.

"No, worse, he'll be at the mercy of his magic. Have you ever seen him lose his temper?"

I recalled that moment he went terminator with the vampires who shunned Georgianna. He nearly killed everyone that day. If it weren't for Karma and my mark —I didn't even want to think about it.

"Once," I said with a shudder. "I think I'd rather face the ogre *and* Chaos again than a pissed-off Monty."

She nodded. "Mages are trained to maintain control at all times. Any strong emotion, any loss of control, can mean disaster or death." She glanced down the corridor Monty had used to enter the facility.

"Well, that explains his exuberant displays of emotion. For a long time I thought he was Vulcan."

A sad smile crossed her lips. "He has profound feelings for those close to him. I just don't think he'll ever allow himself to express those feelings," she said while reaching into her lab coat. "I've been meaning to give this to you. The last time you were here, I was— somewhat preoccupied."

"Ogres and crazed gods have a way of focusing your

attention," I said as she handed me a small, clear crystal the size of a quarter. I took the crystal and laid it on the palm of my hand, examining it carefully. "What's this?" I asked, knowing Roxanne could see the confusion on my face.

"It's a runic lens and it's keyed specifically to Tristan, allowing you to view his energy signature remotely. You can think of it as a magical scanner, non-magic users will be able to see changes through the crystal those of us with magic can see with the naked eye."

"He must be okay. I mean, it's clear." I examined the crystal, turning it around in my hand. "That's good, right?"

She gave me a quick nod. "He's keeping the darkness around him at bay somehow, but it's draining him. If it becomes opaque, you need to bring him to me immediately. Do you carry restraints?"

"Always," I said, opening my coat to show her the pair I kept in an inside pocket. "Why?"

"He'll be back soon. I can't keep him here and there's no reason to while that crystal is clear. He's too stubborn to listen to me. You must keep an eye on him. If the crystal turns red, you have to use the restraints."

I shook my head. "Restraints? On Monty? Are you kidding? I can't do that."

"If you value his friendship, his life, you *will*," she said punctuating each comma with pokes to my chest. "If the crystal turns black, it's too late."

"What happens if it turns black?" I wasn't sure I wanted to hear the answer.

"Do you still carry entropy rounds in Grim Whisper?" she asked, slowly looking away."

Surprised, I nodded. If she knew about my weapon and the entropy rounds, she knew their purpose. I swallowed hard because I knew what her next words were going to be.

"Only for specific situations," I said. "Usually when it's all gone to shit and there's no hope and the world is about to end. You know—the usual."

"If that crystal turns black, the 'usual' will feel like a holiday," she warned.

I clenched my jaw and let out a deep breath. "I'm not going to shoot Monty with entropy rounds." I couldn't believe she would even ask this of me. "I thought you cared for him?"

"More than you'll ever know. But if he goes dark, you'll be able to help stop him. If you don't we won't be around to regret your decision."

FIFTEEN

She made a gesture with her hand and the ambient sounds of the hospital rushed in. I stood silently and put the crystal in my front pocket. I could see Monty coming down the corridor. He looked preoccupied with something.

"Simon, Simon," she said and tapped my shoulder. "Focus."

"I got it," I said quickly, moved to the Goat, and started the engine. "I'll keep an eye on him. Take care of Jimmy."

She nodded as Monty approached. "We will."

"He's sedated and in runic stasis," Monty said, stepping close to Roxanne. "I suggest you keep him that way. We may be dealing with Alder's Permutation or a variant of it."

Roxanne's face darkened. "The Werewolves. Do you know who's doing this? The Permutation is unstable in the best of circumstances. Can you contain it in time?" They walked around the Goat. Monty got in and fastened his seatbelt, then he reached out and held her by the arm, pulling her close.

"Ten layers are good, but I want you to stay near a secure area. We need to go uptown and deal with a situation. Once that's done, we'll find who's doing this and stop them."

"What if you can't contain it? Alder's is a nightmare and if it gets away from the caster we will have the makings of a pandemic."

"If it gets out of control, every Werewolf in the city will transform into a rabid killing machine, and we'll be forced to hunt them down," Monty said calmly as he sat back and sighed, letting go of her.

"Can we go with finding who's responsible and stopping them?" I said, putting the Goat in gear and backing up. "That sounds less fangy."

"Keep your eyes open," Roxanne said, looking at me. "And be safe."

I knew what she meant and felt the weight of the crystal in my pocket as I pulled the Goat out of the bay and headed uptown. I pulled out my phone and speed dialed Ramirez.

"So glad you found the time to call, *pendejo*. You're calling to tell me you're at the cordon and need to get in, right?" Ramirez said quickly.

"Fifteen minutes," I winced as he responded with a loud string of curses in his native Spanish and finished the flurry with a guttural *coño*. Monty raised an eyebrow in admiration.

"If I'm not dead by the time you get here, I'm going to kill you, Simon," Ramirez said after a long sigh. "Is Tristan with you?"

"Yes," I said, feigning insult. "I never hear you threaten *him*."

"I'm crazy, not suicidal. When you get to the scene —call me. Don't breach the containment cordon. We have The Den locked down and the Werewolves trapped inside." He hung up.

"Is he always so cheerful?" Cassandra said from the back and shifted away from the ever-sprawling Peaches. He had reacquired most of the back seat and left her hanging on to the door for balance.

"How long have you known, Ramirez?" I asked, glancing quickly in the rear-view mirror.

"I just transferred over last week from Operations. I wanted to do fieldwork not sit behind a desk." She took her life into her hands by attempting to reclaim some of the back seat by pushing one of Peaches' legs away.

"Sitting behind a desk doesn't get you chomped in half by an angry hellhound," I said, jumping on the West Side Highway and flooring the gas. "And I wouldn't do that, unless you want to be known as 'one-armed Cass.'"

"It's Lieutenant Cassandra, not Cass, or Cassie," she said defiantly, looking at me through the rear-view mirror.

"You move his leg and we'll make sure to get it right on your tombstone. That work for you, Lieutenant *Cassandra*?"

She retracted her hand fast and shot me another look. Peaches rumbled a low growl and a chuff while keeping his head outside the Goat and in the wind as we sped uptown.

"Don't torment her," Monty said and pinched the bridge of his nose with his eyes closed. "She has plenty to take in without you making it worse with that creature."

A rumble was the response from the back.

"She *chose* to be an NYTF Field Agent. I'm sure there's plenty wrong with her thought process."

"Or I'm just not as chickenshit as my peers," she shot back.

"Fear can keep your ass in one piece on this job," I muttered. "Being scared doesn't mean being a coward. It just means you enjoy living."

"How long have you been doing this?" She stared out the window. "Do you get scared?" I heard the unspoken words in her questions. I knew how she felt. There were days I still didn't believe the things I saw.

"Only when I'm awake," I said, glancing back quickly in an effort to reassure her. "It doesn't get easier, but you get tougher."

She placed her hand on her weapon. "We'll see," she said, still looking out into the night as we raced past the Hudson River.

"Monty, what are we looking at and what is this Alder's Mutation you keep referring to?" I gave him a quick sidelong glance. We were about ten minutes away from The Den. I knew once we got there he would jump into the situation.

"It's permutation, not mutation—and it has nothing to do with mutants, before you start your Wolverine rant."

"It's never a rant. We don't take Saint Wolverine's name in vain. Especially if we're about to engage in badassery."

"Alder's Permutation," he continued, ignoring me, "was created by Jeremy Alder, a battle mage. It's designed to force a change against a target. The caster can then control the target after the change."

"Why does that sound bad, especially when dealing with Werewolves?"

"It's not bad—it's horrific. The targets lose their minds, becoming a slave to the caster. It was a fast way to raise an army and decimate enemy numbers."

"This was another one of those wonderful Golden Circle creations, wasn't it?"

He nodded and reached for another power bar. "I told him the spell was too dangerous even with the foci needed. The elders disagreed with me and said it was a necessary evil," he said with thinly veiled anger. "I left the Sanctuary shortly after that."

"What happens to the targets when the spell is removed?" I asked as I swerved around a slow-moving taxi. "Do they go back to normal?"

"The Permutation was designed to be used against enemies in a war. Once the spell runs its course or is removed, the target dies—violently."

"And this…Davros is casting this spell?"

"Not yet, he isn't," he said, finishing his power bar. "He still needs one more foci. The hardest one to get. Although I would've thought the drake's blood was impossible to attain."

"He has the drake's blood and the Phoenix thing. What else does he need?" I said, pulling off to the side. The Den was a block away and I could see the blue flashing lights of the NYTF strobing in the night.

"He needs a conductor for the spell. It was designed to attack a large group at once, not like the negation rune you're familiar with. In order to cast the spell effectively he needs a pound of magically infused platinum."

"That sounds rare."

"It's extremely rare. In my entire life, I never saw more than a few ounces at once. When they first cast the Permutation they pooled the resources of several sects to get the pound needed," he said as I stopped the Goat.

"Then that's good—he can't cast this spell. We find him and take him back to mage jail. Only, this time we use the industrial locks, right?"

"With two of the foci he can cast a variant and release it," he said looking out the window. "It won't be precise but it can still be devastating. There is no control and the targets just run rampant. They become mindless killing machines."

"I'm really starting to dislike mages right about now," I said getting out of the car. I opened the back door and Peaches jumped out and stood next to me. Cassandra got out on the other side. Monty got out and pulled the sleeves of his shirt as he looked up the street.

I placed my hand on the Goat. It locked with a clang and the usual orange glow raced across the surface.

"I never thought I would be facing a Permutation again in my lifetime," Monty said as he began walking to The Den. "Let's go see how bad this is."

SIXTEEN

I hung back and let Cassandra catch up to Monty as I snuck a look at the crystal Roxanne had given me. I let out a sigh of relief when I saw it was still clear. I put it back in my pocket and then looked up the street and noticed the transparent bubble covering the Werewolf club known as The Den.

The building, a repurposed warehouse that once served the now extinct shipping industry, was immense and took up half a city block. It was encased in a shimmering transparent dome of energy. Ramirez walked up to us before we could reach the edge of the cordon.

"Simon, I told you to call me when you got here." He turned to Cassandra. "Where's your cruiser?"

She pointed at Monty but Ramirez glared at me.

"She was about to drive into a minefield of death," I said, raising my hands in surrender. "Monty saved her life. Just couldn't save the cruiser."

"Why am I not surprised? Between the two of you, I go through more vehicles than a demolition derby." He began walking back to what I guessed was the command vehicle. "Stay close and away from that containment field. Last thing I need is more casualties."

I looked around, confused. "What are you talking about? We're fine. Besides, we just got here. How could we be casualties?"

"I never said you were causalities. I said I don't need any more. Collateral damage is something the two of you specialize in. Between his destruction,"—he pointed at Monty—"and you...being *you*, no one, and nothing is safe."

"Well, now that I feel all welcome, why did you call us?" I said while looking at the containment cordon. The surface of the dome coruscated with blue-green energy running across its surface every few seconds.

"How did you get a containment sphere?" Monty asked, admiring the dome as he stepped close. He kept looking up until he almost lost his balance. "And one this big?"

"Our Q-master, Jhon, has been working on amplification tech. Took a regular containment sphere and boosted it somehow," he said, waving a hand. "Science and magic both act the same when it comes to him."

"The Werewolves inside?" Cassandra asked, drawing her weapon. "When are we breaching?"

"*We?* Never," Ramirez answered and pulled her to one side. "If I let something happen to you, your father will kill me."

"I'm a big girl and can handle myself, *Director.* My father will have to live with the fact that he can't control me." She pulled her arm away.

"Doesn't look like *anyone* can do that," I whispered

to Monty, who was still examining the dome. She shot me a dirty look and turned back to Ramirez.

"If she wants to risk maiming or certain death as she bleeds out from catastrophic wounds, I say you let her come," Monty said, and turning to look at Cassandra. "Wouldn't want anyone to think you were—what did you call it? Chickenshit?"

"Catastrophic wounds?" she asked and looked past us at The Den. After a few seconds, she set her jaw and nodded. She had just convinced herself to run into a building inhabited by rabid Werewolves. Clearly, her synapses were misfiring, but I gave her points for badassery. Wolverine would be proud.

"Lieutenant, you don't *have* to do this," I said, getting her attention. "This is some nasty shit and you may not walk out of there."

"I signed up for the nasty shit, Simon, and no one here is going to stop me from taking down those Werewolves." She stepped close and then stopped suddenly as Peaches gave off a low growl. He gave her a look and a low rumble that said 'Please try and attack him so I can remove your legs' and she warily stepped back a few paces.

"Actually, *I* can stop you," Ramirez said, and gestured to the command vehicle. "You'll be monitoring the breach from in there. Surrounded by steel, and agents with guns."

"I can be more helpful inside—" she started.

"Inside the CV," Ramirez continued. "You can provide all kinds of help. These two will be dealing with the threat inside."

She stalked off and headed to the command vehicle.

Once inside, she slammed the door hard enough to shake the entire truck.

"Follow me," Ramirez said with a tired sigh. "We have a secondary CV stationed around the corner."

"Who did you piss off to get her as a lieutenant?" I asked as we followed him to an identical truck.

"Remember the black site we discovered a while back?"

I nodded. The Ferryman, Charon had been trapped in a cell in the detention wing of Haven. We had uncovered a hidden sub-level, which led to a black site. Ramirez reported it to his superiors. Those who were implicated with the secret location were terminated—some permanently. In one stroke, he had single-handedly caused a purge of the NYTF and increased his enemies ten-fold. It catapulted him to director and painted a bullseye on his back.

"Her father is a prick but he's solid," he said as he opened the vehicle doors. "He made sure I came out of that situation intact."

"Director is more than intact; you're running the NYTF," I said following him in with Monty and Peaches behind me. "Now you owe him. This explains your new lieutenant, but active field duty?"

"I wouldn't be here if it weren't for him, so in gratitude I offered to place his daughter in a nice, safe, position behind a desk. Then she went and applied for active field duty. Since then my life is all rainbows and unicorns ever since."

I had to ask. "Why didn't you say no?"

"Have you met my new lieutenant? She was ready to breach a club full of deranged Werewolves—with just her gun and attitude."

"Tell her dad this is a bad idea. Get her reassigned before she gets dead," I said, looking around. The vehicle was full of maps and architectural plans spread out on several small tables.

"Tried that. He's the real old-school type. Pisses acid and spits fire. Got kind of jumpy when your name came up in conversation, by the way." He gave me a strange look that I ignored. He paused a second. When I didn't answer, he continued. "Anyway, he says field duty will be good for her—toughen her up, burn off the dross, and forge her into a real agent. You may know him—George Rott? They called him 'the Rottweiler.'"

It explained a lot about the lieutenant. George 'Rottweiler' Rott was one of the best special ops team leaders. Meticulous and flexible. His missions were still being studied in the NYTF academy.

"She's her father's daughter then—my condolences. Are these the plans to the club?" I said, trying to change the subject. My time and what I did in the NYTF had been erased from every record for good reason. No one outside of Monty knew what I did when I'd served there. I planned to keep it that way. It didn't stop Ramirez from trying to figure it out, though.

Ramirez nodded and shuffled some of the large rolls off the table. He unrolled one set of plans and pointed to a set of tunnels that ran under the club.

"You've got to be kidding," I leaned closer, studying the plans. Monty leaned in too and then stepped back with a look of disgust.

"I need some tea if you're having us breach through sewers, treading through that foul stench," Monty muttered as he stepped away from the table and sat in one of the large desk chairs.

Ramirez looked at me. "Is he serious? He wants tea —now? It's the middle of the night," he said in disbelief.

"He never jokes about tea time, and any time is tea time—trust me on this, just get the tea. Earl Grey, no sugar, make sure it's brewed well."

Ramirez nodded to one of the agents, who exited the command vehicle in search of tea, and then he smoothed out the plans on the table. "It's not a sewer line. These are old smuggler tunnels that lead from the club directly to the pier."

"How do we access them?" I asked, following the plans. "It looks like they come up in the center of the club?"

"The basement of the building next door leads you to the club's basement," Ramirez said, tracing the tunnel with a finger. "It brings you up in the middle, but you shouldn't be seen it's been sealed for decades."

A few minutes later, the agent returned carrying a steaming cup, which he handed to Monty. He nodded his thanks, then leaned back and inhaled the aroma for a moment before taking a sip, closing his eyes, and groaning in satisfaction.

"He *really* enjoys his tea," Ramirez said, glancing at Monty.

"He's English. It's in his DNA and it's obscene. Any agents coming with us, or is this just Monty and me?"

"I can't spare any more men on a frontal assault, but

I can give you backup. Once you get inside and engage the Werewolves, we'll breach through the back and try to catch them off-guard."

I shook my head in disbelief. "So we're the distraction *and* bait? For a moment I thought you didn't care. I want dinner at *Kurumazushi*, forget Luger's. And it'd better be the *omakase* experience, *Director*."

"You take care of this without me losing any more men, or vehicles, and I'll get you a seat at Masa, on me," Ramirez said, his face serious. I don't know what impressed me more—that he knew about Masa or that he offered to buy me a dinner that cost upwards of four hundred dollars. "I called you because you two are the best at this."

Monty stood up and walked to the doors. "Now that the menu is settled, can we go see about these Werewolves?" he said and left the command vehicle.

"Is he in a bad mood or something?" Ramirez asked.

"He doesn't do good moods. I think he breaks out in a rash when he tries to smile. A good mood may put him in the hospital," I said following Monty out of the vehicle. Peaches trailed behind me. I crouched down and rubbed behind his ears. "You stay here and guard Ramirez. I'll be back soon."

He gave me a low growl and a bump with his head that was just this side of rib-cracking. I caught my breath, stood up and headed over to the entrance of the abandoned warehouse that connected to the club. I checked Grim Whisper, tightened my thigh sheath, holding Ebonsoul, and made sure the mala was accessible. I gave Monty a quick look. He nodded and I pushed open the door.

SEVENTEEN

A musty smell rushed to greet us as we entered the darkness of the warehouse. Monty cast a spell and an orb of light floated above us, illuminating the space. It tracked with us as we crossed the large open area to the stairs going down. Puddles of stagnant water dotted the floor. The hairs on the nape of my neck stood on end and I turned quickly to look behind me. For a second it felt like someone was staring at me.

"What is it?" Monty asked at my sudden movement.

"Nothing," I peered into the darkness, still feeling uneasy. "I thought I felt someone behind me—staring."

"Where? Show me where the feeling came from."

"Monty, it's just nerves. We're about to face a group of angry psycho Werewolves. My common sense is just freaking out a bit—okay, a lot."

"Show me where," he repeated, his voice tight.

I pointed to the wall behind us and to the right. He stepped close to the wall and gestured. Runes flared in the air before him. "Shite," he muttered under his breath and crossed the floor back to my side. "That gobshite, Beck, summoned a Lurk."

"Which is…?" I looked back at the wall where I felt the presence.

"Think of it as magical surveillance. Lurks live in the shadows. They watch and report back to the caster whatever the target is doing and saying."

"Why is it watching me? Isn't Beck after you?"

"I would have sensed it earlier. Actually, I'm surprised you felt it. Your magical ability is growing," he said, approaching the stairs.

"No thanks. I don't want extra magical ability. I don't want any magical ability." I looked back up quickly as we descended the stairs. "Aren't you going to, you know, cast some Lurk-remover or something?"

"They are notoriously difficult to eliminate. I really don't want to waste the energy on it, but let me know if you feel that sensation of being watched again," he said, and then pointed. "Over there."

At the other end of the basement, I could just make out a steel door. As we approached, I could tell from the dust and cobwebs that no one had been down here in years.

"That door hasn't been used in decades, from the look of it. Maybe we should get some of the NYTF down here?"

"Too noisy. We'll lose the element of surprise." He shook out his hands, closed his eyes and rubbed his hands together slowly, keeping the fingers extended. Twenty seconds later, he separated them and a thin disc of water floated in front of him. He rotated his hands and the disc turned on its side. With a word whispered under his breath, the disc turned and became a blur. He walked close to the door hinges and released it.

The disc cut silently through the hinges in seconds, reminding me of a high-pressure water jet in action. He turned it to follow the doorframe and the door began to fall forward. With another gesture, a cushion of air caught the door and gently eased it down before it hit the floor.

"Have I told you how scary you can be?" I whispered, looking at the door on the ground in amazement.

"Says the man who is immortal, can stop time, and speaks to the embodiment of causality on a regular basis," he said, turning to me with a rare smile. He gestured to the tunnel, and added, "Shall we?"

"Monty, wait." I pulled out the crystal Roxanne had given me. It was still clear as I held it between my thumb and forefinger. "Roxanne gave me this because your energy signature is jacked. She thinks you may have gone dark, or are on your way."

"I know." He looked at me with the hint of another rare smile. "Thank you for telling me. She means well, but she has no idea what's going on."

"What do you mean? Wait, you knew? We were in a sphere of silence and you were checking on Jimmy. How could you know?"

He cocked his head to one side. "She gave you a crystal designed to track and monitor my magical wellbeing. How do you think it does that?"

"Shit, it draws on your power, doesn't it?" I said, holding the crystal and examining it. I decided not to mention Roxanne's suggestions about the restraints, or putting entropy bullets into him if he got out of control.

He nodded. "Every few seconds it does a 'pull' on me. It's not a siphon, but I feel it the same way you'd feel an ant crawling on your arm. Sensing energy pulls is one of the first things we are trained in as mages," he said glancing at me. "But that's not your real question, is it?"

I shook my head slowly and looked into his eyes. "Have you gone dark?" I asked, letting my hand rest on Grim Whisper. "I need to know you have whatever this is under control. I saw the black circle around your energy."

"What you saw was a timed-release erasure," he said with a sigh. "If it were an accurate representation, my energy orb should be diminishing. It looks similar to when a mage goes dark, except black invades the orb."

"The explosion—Beck," I said, realizing what he meant when he said his work was done. "Wait, Beck said he saw something off with your signature, before the explosion, and so did Roxanne the last time we went to Haven. She said she couldn't sense your signature."

He nodded and entered the tunnel. "I've been masking my presence for some time now." He stepped around some of the puddles. "It makes me hard to read or locate, like scrambling a GPS. Masking, however, left me vulnerable to the erasure."

I followed him in and drew Grim Whisper. He cast another orb of light and it floated in front of us.

"Should you be doing that—using magic?"

"Do you have a flashlight?"

"No, not with me," I said, remembering I did have one back in the Goat. "I left it in the bag."

"Then I need to use magic if you want to see. Unless you prefer wandering around this tunnel in the dark?"

"No, thank you. How long before you're erased?" The question seemed absurd.

"There's a way to reverse this, but for that I'm going

to need William or a mage at his level. He's better at masking than I ever was. This means we need to find Davros. I'm certain William is tracking him to prevent the Permutation."

"You need to find your brother, who you thought was dead, but isn't, to stop Davros, who seems to be deranged? Well, this just gets better by the second. You never answered my question. How long before you're 'Monty the magic-less mage'?"

"That's not even remotely funny," he said while brushing some hair out of his face. "I don't know. If that crystal goes opaque, the erasure has begun. If it turns red I may have anywhere from a few hours to a few days."

"She said if it goes black it's too late," I said, looking down the tunnel and seeing the door to the Werewolf club. "We're here."

"If it goes black, my power and abilities are gone." He placed his hand on the steel surface. Frowning, he added, "This door has been used recently."

"How recently?"

"I can't tell. Something is blocking it, maybe the containment. Are you ready?"

I drew Ebonsoul, heaved a breath, and nodded. "Let's shut this down."

He pushed the door and we stepped into the basement of The Den. The orb illuminated the space, which appeared to be empty. The door to the tunnel slammed closed behind us. Runes around the doorframe flared a bright red, sealing us in.

"Time to die, humans," said a voice echoing all around us.

"I thought you said we had the element of surprise? He doesn't sound surprised," I whispered, trying to get a bead on where the voice was coming from.

"It's obvious they were expecting some kind of assault," Monty said forming an orb of fire in his hand. "Did Ramirez say how many Werewolves were in the club?"

"He said he was dealing with three of them. Why?"

Monty closed his eyes for a second. "There are a lot more than three Werewolves in this club."

"How many more?" I said, looking around the basement.

"Enough to make this a bad idea. Did you pack the runed silver ammo?"

"Yes, and brought some of the entropy in case we run into any more of your friends. The only exit just sealed itself, didn't it?"

He nodded. "We'll have to use one of the other exits upstairs if we want to get out of here."

"So much for the element of surprise," I said as a werewolf shimmered into view. "Fuck, what did we just walk into? Since when do they camouflage?"

"It's the Permutation. It's changing their abilities."

I checked Grim Whisper, making sure the rounds were in it. "Have I told you how much mages suck?" I paused, looking over at him. "Present company excluded."

"You may have mentioned it once or twice," he said as he created another orb of white-hot flame. "I can't say I disagree right now."

The Werewolf growled and then laughed.

"Tristan, it really has been too long." Its voice was

unnervingly normal sounding, making it difficult for me to reconcile what I was hearing with what I was seeing.

"Friend of yours?" I asked, looking at Monty.

"Davros," Monty said, ignoring me. "Not long enough. How are you controlling it? The Permutation is not complete."

"I don't need a full Permutation to control these stupid aberrations. Once transformed, their minds are reduced to simple impulses of killing and feeding—impulses I intend to exploit."

"You were erased and placed under observation. How did you escape?"

"Observation? Is that what you're calling it now? Stripping me of my power and incarcerating me? Me? Your sect brother! We fought side-by-side, Tristan!"

"You became unstable. What you did...We had no choice," Monty whispered. "Your powers had to be erased."

"Speaking of erased," —Davros narrowed his eyes —"how are you feeling? From the looks of things you don't have much time."

"Enough time to deal with you."

Davros laughed again, the sound bouncing off the stone walls and amplifying.

"You don't understand. This club is full of Werewolves under my control. I let that incompetent outside think he was dealing with only three of them. There's ten times that amount upstairs. You aren't leaving here alive."

"Why are you doing this, Davros?"

"I would tell you to ask your brother, but you won't

live long enough for that. Goodbye, Tristan."

The Werewolf fell to the floor and convulsed.

"I'm going to take a wild guess that whoever was controlling it—this Davros—isn't a fan of yours," I said, looking at the Werewolf writhe and twist on the floor.

"His mind is gone, but the rage remains. Always a bad sign."

The Werewolf flipped from side to side. Blood began flowing from its eyes, ears, and mouth.

"That…doesn't look normal, Monty. What the hell?"

"Davros is leaving the body and giving up control. Once he leaves it completely, the Werewolf will attack."

I checked Grim Whisper again and made sure I still had a round in the chamber.

"Can't I just shoot it now while it's busy on the floor doing…whatever it is that it's doing?" I took aim. "Would save us the whole avoiding being 'slashed in two' thing."

Monty shook his head and began tracing runes. "If you shoot it while transitioning, the rounds will be ineffective. The Permutation makes them resistant to the effects of magic and silver. Once Davros leaves, it should be vulnerable."

"What are you doing?"

"Dealing with more than thirty Werewolves without killing them."

"I hope this method involves our staying alive," I said looking at the runes float into the wall. "Is that like a magical flea spell? Something to keep them occupied while we escape?"

"We have to stop Davros before he decimates the

Werewolves." His hands were moving too fast for me to follow. "His xenophobia thrived during the war. He's motivated by a blind rage against anything not human."

"And you called this guy your friend?"

Monty paused for a second and looked at me.

"He wasn't always that way. The war twisted him. He lost everything...everyone," he whispered and resumed sending runes out. "We have to protect the Werewolves."

"Because we love Werewolves so much?"

"Because imbalances in the power structure will destabilize the Council. The other supernaturals will sense their vulnerability and move in to capitalize on their weakness."

"A supernatural civil war—shit. That would be bad."

"Quite, since it wouldn't remain confined to the supernatural population for long."

"How do we stop this? Can you sense Davros?"

He pointed at the Werewolf. "I think we have more pressing matters at the moment." It had stopped convulsing and was now on all fours.

It stood slowly, and it looked angry.

"This is where the 'mindless killing machine' kicks in, isn't it?"

Monty nodded and formed orbs of white-hot flame in his hands. "We can't save him. The Permutation has destroyed his mind. He's dead as soon as he transforms back."

"And the ones upstairs?" I said raising Grim Whisper.

"We can still save those, if they're not too far gone."

This Werewolf was a promise of death. It crouched

down, every muscle coiled and ready to strike. Drool mixed with blood trickled down from its fangs. It shook its head and raked a claw against the stone wall, causing sparks to shower to the floor. It looked around, confused, as it sniffed the air. Once it caught our scent, it howled.

This wasn't the howl you heard on those nature specials, either, where it seems the wolves are simply homesick and are calling out to their pack in a soulful yearning. This was the 'freeze your blood to subzero, your ass is dead, you may as well make peace with your maker' howl. I'd never been scared shitless until that moment.

Several howls answered in a chorus of impending death and maiming. I heard the footfalls of the Werewolves upstairs crash onto the floor above us.

The Werewolf roared and lunged at us as Monty released the orbs.

EIGHTEEN

Werewolves were killing machines. Razor-sharp claws, lightning-fast reflexes, heightened senses, and a mouth full of fangs gave them a few options on how they could tear you to shreds. Add to that the denser skin and a high tolerance for pain, and you're looking at a very bad moment with a short life expectancy.

All of that pales, though, in comparison to a pissed-off mage.

One orb hit the Werewolf square in the chest and

reacted like napalm. The fire spread as the Werewolf landed and swiped at Monty. He leaped to the side and unleashed the other orb. It engulfed the Werewolf in flames.

"This would be a good time to use your weapon," Monty said as he ducked under another swipe, placing a hand on the floor. Blue lines of power raced toward the Werewolf as I unloaded the rounds from Grim Whisper into its chest. It staggered back, regained its balance, and snarled.

"Silver rounds are doing squat, even the runed ones. I'm open to ideas, Monty." I rolled away from a slash meant to remove my midsection. "I could switch out for entropy rounds but that means it gets messy."

"Too dangerous inside this containment dome. Plus, I don't know if traces of the Permutation will affect the rounds adversely, creating a singularity and swallowing us all."

"No entropy rounds—got it," I said quickly as I pushed off the wall and slid across the floor, away from a series of slashes. "That fire isn't slowing him down."

He formed another orb of flame and used it to block the Werewolf's path. "You need to use the blade. It will work against it."

"I knew you were going to say that," I said, shaking my head as I stood back up. "You know I hate using the blade."

"My magic is having little effect outside of angering it further," he said as the Werewolf approached. "If you don't want to use your blade, maybe you could have a conversation using stern language, like the way you speak to your creature?"

"His name is Peaches and your humor never ceases to inspire," I holstered Grim Whisper and switched Ebonsoul to my other hand. I held the main bead of the mala between my fingers.

"Just remember what Yat taught you and you should come out of this mostly whole. Cover your eyes," Monty said, releasing the orb. It slammed into the Werewolf's face and flashed.

Master Yat's words rushed into the forefront of my mind as I entered a defensive stance against my impending dismemberment.

"When using a weapon, make no distinction where the weapon begins and you end. Become one."

"Sounds like something I would read in a fortune cookie. Followed by: my lucky numbers are 11, 34, 65 etc.," I managed to say, right before his stick peppered my ribs with several strikes, lighting up my world in a wonderful spectrum of pain.

"See? Weapon and wielder are one. Intention and action are the same. How do your ribs feel?" he asked with a smile.

"Battered, bruised, and beaten," I said, gasping through the pain.

"Good. That is called an object lesson. I used this object"—he held up his stick— "to teach you a lesson. Begin the drill again."

I held Ebonsoul in a reverse grip with the blade out and leaped forward. Above us, I could hear a muffled explosion. Ramirez was starting his breach. We needed to move fast. The NYTF agents would be shredded when they realized that "three" was really over thirty Werewolves in the club.

Twisting away from a rake meant to remove my throat, I stepped close—closer than I wanted—and pressed the bead on the mala. It slammed the Werewolf against the wall with enough force to shatter some of the stone. I followed with a slash of my own, slicing through the Werewolf's neck and nearly removing its head. The effect was immediate. It fell back, grabbing its throat as it transformed to human form. The body twitched for a few seconds and then went still.

Ebonsoul siphoned the energy to me, and my vision tunneled in. I ran up the stairs with Monty right behind me.

The door at the top of the stairs and blew off its hinges as I charged through. Three Werewolves surrounded me as I slid into the main floor. I could smell many more all around me. They needed to die. I wanted them to die. I saw a figure run in front of me and slam a hand into the floor. Blue light filled the room and the world disappeared.

NINETEEN

The pain crushed me, and I gasped as I opened my eyes to the blinding light. My brain felt like it was trying to crawl out of my skull and was succeeding. I opened my mouth to say something and instantly regretted it. My jaw hurt and my stomach did flip-flops as a wave of nausea vise-gripped me. Every part of my body ached. I saw Monty standing off to the side, talking to one of the NYTF agents, as EMTe workers fussed over me.

"EMTe" stood for EMT elite. The NYTF used these paramedics whenever they encountered some kind of supernatural disaster, or when Monty was allowed to run rampant, which was pretty much the same thing. They all wore dark red uniforms and drove around in extra-large blue ambulances.

They were the Navy Seals of the paramedics. Tough as two-day-old steak, and willing to risk their lives no matter the situation. Some of them had magical healing ability, and they all possessed a certain 'sensitivity' to supernatural phenomena.

I had become a widely discussed topic among the EMTe community given my peculiar 'condition.' Most of them took it in stride, giving me space and time to let my body heal itself. Others, the rookies, always tried to help me, only to be shocked when I recuperated before their eyes from something that should have killed me.

It was a small group and I knew most of them.

"How bad is it, Frank?" I croaked, my throat raw.

Frank defined grizzled older, mid-sixties, built like a wall and probably as tough. He was the oldest EMTe still in the field and was affectionately known as the OG. I thought it meant "old gangsta," but one of the other EMTe told me it meant "original geezer."

"You got second-degree burns all over your body, which is probably why you feel like hell," he said around the unlit cigar in his mouth. "Your head should feel like it was used for soccer practice and your stomach should be twisted up in knots."

I nodded. "Yeah, what the hell hit me? I remember coming through the door, being surrounded by

Werewolves, and then a blue flash."

"Surprised you remember anything at all," he said packing up his bag. "You were hit with an electrical charge large enough to fry an elephant. I'm going to guess that was Tristan, who, by the way, refused to let me examine him."

"He'll be fine, just give him a few minutes," Monty said and brushed the hair out of his face before looking at me. "Feeling chipper, are we?"

Frank shook his head as he headed out of the club. "Don't know why I bother with you two. Try to keep it to one disaster tonight. I don't want to see your faces for a few days, if possible."

"You look like shit," Ramirez said, crouching into my field of vision.

Monty was pulled off to the side again, into another conversation with an NYTF agent. I could see some of the agents loading the Werewolves onto gurneys, assisted by more of the EMTe.

"Feel like it, too," I croaked as I tried to sit up.

Another EMTe rested a hand on my chest and shook his head. "A few more minutes, Mr. Strong."

"I don't know how he did it," Ramirez whispered, sneaking a glance at Monty. "He stopped them all. But he looks almost as bad as you do. You'd better get him checked out. He didn't let Frank look at him and he won't listen to me."

I looked over to where Monty stood. I fished in my pocket for the crystal. It had turned a smoky gray. He saw me and gave me an almost imperceptible shake of the head before returning to his conversation.

"Shit," I said and moved again to sit up. The EMTe

closed in to stop me and I gave him my best glare.
Behind me, I heard a familiar growl and I smiled. "If
you don't want my puppy to use your hand as a chew-
toy, I wouldn't do that."

He backed off. "Puppy? That thing is a puppy?" He
packed his things and moved quickly after Frank.

"He's not a thing," I called out after him. "His name
is Peaches." I turned and rubbed his head for a few
seconds before I wobbled to my feet. "Good boy.
Thanks for keeping an eye on Ramirez."

<I'm hungry. Can I bite one of the bad dogs?>

I turned my head sharply, wincing in pain as my
skull felt squeezed and my vision tunneled, and tried to
focus on Ramirez.

"What did you say?" I asked, surprised, since
Ramirez didn't speak with an English accent and
Monty was still speaking to the agent.

"I didn't say anything," Ramirez said giving me a
concerned look. "Maybe you *should* lie down. Especially
if you're hearing voices."

I looked down at Peaches, who cocked his head to
one side.

"No, we need to get out of here. I'll take Monty to
Haven and make sure he gets looked at."

I looked over at Monty and caught his eye. With a
gentler motion of my head, I let him know we needed
to leave.

Ramirez grabbed my hand. "Hey, Strong, thanks for
the assist. If you guys hadn't come through—I would
have lost more agents. Masa, on me, as soon as you
stop hearing voices and act normal."

"You'd better believe I'm taking you up on that," I

said while heading for the front door. Blocking it stood an angry Cassandra. I let Peaches get ahead of me and she stepped to the side. "Excuse me, Lieutenant."

My body was recovering and the aches were fading with each step. She glared at me but kept her distance.

"A fake CV," she said and rested her hand on her holster, looking down at Peaches. "Ramirez thinks he's funny, but I *will* get in the field. He can't keep me out of the action forever."

I turned to her, suddenly angry. "You're so busy rushing *into* the action that you don't see he's just trying to keep you alive."

The Den was a hive of activity. I looked around at the NYTF and EMTe moving back and forth and securing the site. By daybreak they would be gone, as if nothing had happened.

"You got out okay," she said defiantly. "It couldn't have been *that* bad."

"It wasn't *that* bad, if you overlook the fact that I should be dead," I said, leaving her fuming at the entrance of the club.

Monty caught up with me when I got to the car. I was feeling better, but still achy. I placed my hand on the Goat, and it opened with a clang. I opened the back door, and Peaches bounded into the back and sprawled. I slid into the driver's side and closed my eyes. Monty reached for a power bar.

"How bad is it?" I asked without opening my eyes. "How far along?"

He looked away. "I'm fine. I may have overextended myself a bit, but I'll be fine. I just need rest."

"Overextended? Damn it, Monty, you fried the

entire club! How the hell did you even do that?"

"I tapped into the containment dome, and reworked its properties to emit a large pulse when I activated it. Similar to a magical EMP."

"That was the blue flash," I said, pulling out the crystal. It was still a smoky gray. "This doesn't look good, Monty. I need to get you to Roxanne."

"We don't have time. We need to find Davros before he infects more Werewolves. If he managed to infect so many at once, he is close to completing the Permutation. We can't let that happen."

"The crystal is gray, do you see this?" I held it up in front of his face. "It's gray. It was clear and now it's gray. Gray is bad."

"As long as I don't over-use my abilities I will be fine. Let's go investigate this 'island of siblings' the drake spoke about. The sooner we stop Davros the better. Head uptown. Take the FDR."

"Where is this island?" I swerved the Goat around as we drove down to 42nd Street to cross the city. "I've never heard of any 'sibling island' in New York, and I've lived here my entire life."

"Don't you think it's time you fed your creature? I don't relish the thought of a hungry hellhound running loose, much less in the back of the car." He looked back at Peaches. "You didn't bring dog food?"

"You know he doesn't eat dog food, despite what Hades said. You don't remember the last time I tried to give him dog food?"

"Wasn't that a stainless steel bowl?"

I nodded. "He bit right through it and then spit out the pieces at me."

<It was insulting. I don't know how you call that food. I'm sure you wouldn't eat it.>

I swerved to one side and almost lost control of the Goat.

"What's wrong?" Monty said, alarmed.

"You didn't hear that?"

Monty raised an eyebrow at me.

"Hear what?" he said, slowly looking around. "What did you hear?"

"That voice, it sounded like you, only less refined. It sounded like that guy from that movie, Lock, Stock, and a Barrel of Monkeys?"

"You mean, *Lock, Stock and Two Smoking Barrels*?"

"That one! The scary guy who smashed the head into the car—him."

"You're hearing Vinnie Jones in your head? Maybe we do need to go to Haven. It's clear you have a concussion."

"I know what I heard. Last time it mentioned being hungry. I'm not imagining it."

"Last time? How many times have you heard Vinnie Jones? Is he appearing to you in your sleep? Do you see him now?" He looked in the back again. Peaches rumbled and I swear it sounded like laughter.

"Oh, hilarious. I never said I saw him, just heard his voice, and I know what I heard and—oh shit." I saw a fireball racing down the street chasing us.

TWENTY

"Monty, can we do something about the large fireball coming this way? You know, the inferno chasing us?"

"I wonder…" he said, rubbing his chin. "Do you think Vinnie Jones cast that fireball at us?"

"So not funny!" I said as I swerved. The fireball changed direction to track us. It was closing even as I stepped on the gas.

He stuck his head out the window and looked behind us. "Don't bother trying to outrun it, Simon. It's moving too fast."

"What do you suggest? I let it hit us?" I asked feeling a little panicked. Images of being barbequed in the Goat flashed before my eyes. It wasn't pretty.

"Actually, yes." He shook out his hands. "Stop the car. She's been following us since The Den."

"Are you serious?"

"Yes, stop the car but don't get out," He said his voice tight. "And keep your creature inside as well. I'm going to have to convince her to leave the city—or dispatch her."

I stopped the Goat and kept my eyes on the rear-view mirror. The fireball's flames increased in size as it got closer. It punched into us, and the interior of the Goat flashed orange as the flames washed over the surface of the car. They dissipated a few seconds later as runes floated through the car.

"What was that?" I said, surprised.

"Cecil calls it the Ziller Effect. It takes magical attacks, breaks them down into their respective components, and redirects the recompostioned energy —and I've lost you, haven't I?" He shook his head.

"You lost me at Ziller Effect. Looks like it works,

though, since we're still here to discuss it, even though you almost melted my brain trying to explain it."

"I figured it would make sense to protect the car from supernatural attacks. It's runed against practically everything—including dragons." He stepped out of the car. In the distance, I could see a figure running at us.

I pulled out Grim Whisper and stepped out. The figure shimmered and for a second it disappeared. Moments later a large dragon raced at us. It was Slif.

"What does she want?" I said, checking Grim Whisper to make sure I had entropy rounds loaded. "I thought she was on our side?"

"I think the fireball made it clear what she wants, and dragons only have one side—theirs," he said and stepped forward, flexing his fingers. Peaches materialized next to my leg a second later. "So much for the two of you staying in the car."

"Is she bigger now, or am I imagining that?" I asked, admiring the large creature advancing on us. This time she had wings that spanned the entire width of the street. "She grew wings?"

Watching her, I understood why dragons were feared and revered all throughout history. Seeing one up close was a fearsome and beautiful thing. Heavy on the fearsome side.

"She was never small. She just assumed that size to deceive us. Isn't that right, dragon?" he asked the looming creature. Slif took several steps to the side, cracking the pavement and street, doing her best Smaug impression.

"How did you deflect the Permutation?" Slif asked and whipped her tail around. I leaped out of the way, followed by Monty. Peaches pounced and bit down on it. Slif whipped her tail around again and launched Peaches across the street, through a storefront window, into a clothing store.

He stalked outside seconds later, his eyes glowing red. A lacy white G-string hung haphazardly from one ear. It sailed across the sidewalk as he gave his head a good shake. I made a mental note never to piss him off, aware of the fact that the likelihood of it occurring accidentally was inevitable.

"It's not complete," Monty said, getting to his feet and brushing off the dirt. "You're here to make sure that happens, aren't you? Did you lie about my brother? Is William really alive?"

"The dealings of dragons are beyond you, mage," Slif hissed, moving around us. She resembled a snake —a large, red, fire-breathing snake. "I owe you no explanation and offer none except death."

"Pretty weak as far as explanations go." I fired Grim Whisper, emptying the magazine. She opened her mouth and exhaled. A blast of super-heated air intercepted and incinerated the entropy rounds before they reached her.

I jumped behind the Goat as she turned her head to face me, melting the sidewalk where I'd stood seconds earlier. The surface of the Goat flared bright orange, and then reverted to its normal purple after a few seconds. Aside from being warm to the touch, it was unscathed. I was really beginning to love this car, despite the fact that it resembled a giant grape.

"You will leave this city or I *will* destroy you," Monty said with his head bowed and arms extended. "Do not force this, Slif."

Slif roared and laughed. "You overestimate your ability, mage. You have neither the power nor the ability in your current state to stop me or issue threats."

I saw her take a deep breath. The kind of breath children take right before they blow out birthday candles. It was the 'cheeks puffed out and lungs filled to capacity' kind of breath. Then I felt Monty huddle beside me behind the Goat.

This caused me a moment of confusion as I looked over the hood. There was Monty across the street, doing his best 'You shall not pass' Gandalf impersonation, *and* yet he was also next to me, getting into the Goat. I was seeing two Montys, and for a second my brain did a backflip.

"Get in the car," he said and strapped the seatbelt around his body. "She's right, and in ten seconds when she blasts that illusion she will turn her attention to the real me."

"We're running?" I scrambled over to the driver's side and got in. "Not that I mind, if it means staying in one piece. What happened to 'I will destroy you' and that pose? Even I was tempted to surrender."

"Indomitable in retreat, invincible in advance," he said, making a few gestures and ducking back out of sight. "Right now we're doing the retreat part. Once she blasts that illusion, you take off. Not before or we'll be done."

"Didn't Churchill also say 'We shall never surrender'?"

"This is a strategic retreat, not surrender," he said. "Call your creature and be ready to leave in a hurry."

He put his hands together and closed his eyes in concentration.

"How am I supposed to call him?" I looked out the window as the fake Monty raised his arms and formed two orbs of orange flame in his hands.

"A little busy at the moment," he said without opening his eyes. "You're the one bonded to it. Figure it out and get ready to go."

I tried the only thing I could think of. I could feel my brow crease as I tried hard to project my thought towards him.

Hey, boy, we need to go—now! Come back to the car before this dragon barbecues us all.

Seconds later, Peaches materialized in the back seat with a low rumble.

<I had her right where I wanted her.>

"Are you kidding me? She threw you through a window!" I said aloud, looking behind me. I turned to see Monty open one eye and close it again.

"Vinnie Jones again?"

"It's Peaches, I swear," I said, giving Peaches the stink-eye, which he ignored.

"Of course it is. I would appreciate a bit of quiet. Could you relay the message to Mr. Jones?"

The engine purred as I waited, my foot hovering over the gas pedal, and sweat forming on my brow. As fake-Monty brought his arms back to launch the fireballs, Slif exhaled a blast of blue flame and I stepped on the gas, screeching away.

My foot had the pedal to the floor and we were standing still. Around us, everything that wasn't secure was being sucked in. Slif screamed as a black vortex formed around her and held her in place. She flapped her wings furiously but didn't move.

"Monty is that…is that a black hole?" I asked, fear forcing me to press down on the pedal harder. A cloud of smoke formed around us as the rubber of the tires burned.

His hands were gesturing wildly. "It's a void vortex, and we seem to be a bit too close. We may need an added push. Could you activate your shield?"

"Isn't that what Beck told you *not* to do?" I asked as I accessed the mala. "The thing that the Golden Circle would be upset about?"

"No, this is worse. A void vortex is very much like a magical wormhole. It connects two points, shunting everything through it instantly. Including the dragon. This one connects to Siberia."

"Siberia, Russia?" I asked, shocked.

"I didn't know there was another. I would have sent her to Antarctica if I knew how. This will definitely get the Circle's attention."

I glanced back at the trapped dragon. "Won't the cold kill her?"

"Your concern for the creature that tried to incinerate you a scant few minutes ago is touching. The cold will be the least of our worries if we don't get away from here. The shield, please."

I pressed the main bead. The shield formed but nothing happened. Monty placed his hand in the shield and muttered something under his breath. The shield disappeared and the Goat took off. The needle on the speedometer dropped to the right and stayed there, vibrating in place. I looked behind us and saw Slif still stuck in place, receding fast.

"We're running out of road and we're going too fast. The sudden stop is going to be lethal," I gripped the wheel until my knuckles turned white, not daring to turn for fear of flipping us over.

"Working…on it," Monty said, his voice strained. "Just need a moment."

He placed his hands on the dashboard and began speaking in a language I didn't understand. I figured he was giving us our last rites, since the Goat wasn't slowing down.

"When I tell you, apply the brakes," he said as sweat poured off his face and he gritted his teeth.

I suddenly felt an intense pressure on my body and the Goat began slowing down.

"Now, Simon, brakes!" he yelled and then grunted as I pushed down on the brake. The Goat slowed down and rolled to a stop as we crossed 1st Avenue. I saw the East River several hundred feet ahead of us. I peeled my fingers from the wheel and looked outside. I let out the breath I had been unconsciously holding as my heart continued doing an Irish jig in my chest.

"Monty, that was shay—" I started with a smack on the wheel.

He held up a hand. "No. Don't you dare use that adjective to describe what I just did. I swear I'll feed you to the dragon."

"We were going fast enough to cut the Kessel Run to less than ten parsecs. How did you stop the Goat?"

"I increased the mass of the vehicle until Newton's third law kicked in and slowed us down. The same law applies to the vortex and the dragon." He looked down the street. "The more she resists, the more it will act on her and pull her in."

"Speaking of dragon...How long will your black hole hold it? Can't imagine rush hour with a dragon trapped on 42nd Street and Lex. Dawn is only a few hours away."

"The vortex will transport her shortly, but she will be back in a few days. We need to find Davros before then. When she gets back, she will be livid." He got out of the car, and leaned against it. "I need a moment to catch my breath."

"What I *need* is coffee. I wonder if Crutch has the Last Gasp open" I searched in my pocket and pulled out the crystal. It had become an onyx gem, and my breath caught in my chest. "Shit—Monty..."

I looked up in time to see Monty collapse on the street. A second later, the crystal shattered in my hand.

TWENTY-ONE

Roxanne was nearly hysterical as Monty was wheeled into the emergency room. "I told you to bring him to me when it turned red, and you waited until it became black and shattered? I thought you were his *friend?*"

I let her vent up to this point because I knew she was worried, but no one questioned my loyalty, *ever*.

"I'm not his friend, I'm his family. You ever doubt that again, and you and I are going to have a serious problem," I said with quiet menace. Peaches rumbled next to me in agreement. "Are we clear?"

<I could remove one of her legs. Just say the word.>

I gave him a quick shake of my head in response.

"Simon, I'm sorry. It's just that this is critical. I'm not a mage, and I've not dealt with this type of damage or an erasure spell. I'm out of my depth here." The words had tumbled out as tears fell down her face. She wiped them away and composed herself. "I'm a bloody mess and I can't help him. I need a mage a powerful one and we don't have one of those on staff."

I pulled out my phone. "I know where to find one."

"That's not funny, and it's in poor taste, Simon," she said, gesturing at my phone. "You have another mage's phone number in there?"

"No, but I have the number of someone who knows where a powerful mage is. How soon do you need this mage?"

"Twenty-four hours, forty-eight on the outside. After that I don't know. I just don't— if we don't get this reversed he may lose his ability to cast."

"Got it. Two days max. Don't know why I thought this would be easy. I'm dealing with Monty, after all. I'll be back before then. Keep him stable." I gave her a nod and then ran out of Haven.

I made the call outside the facility. It rang twice and connected.

"Strong, why are you calling me? Wait—how did you even get this number?"

"Ken, did you find her? The psycho-mage from The Randy Rump? Did you find Quan?"

"Do you realize it's almost dawn?" he said, his voice thick from impending sleep. Vampires couldn't resist the onset of dawn without their bodies shutting down.

"I'm going to bed. Don't call me again."

"You're right, I'll just call Chi and explain how you let the mage responsible for the infected Werewolves get away so you can take a nap."

It was a bluff. Quan wasn't the mage responsible, but he didn't know that.

"Are you threatening me," he replied, his voice suddenly clear, "with my own sister?"

"Where is the mage? This is important."

"It must be if we are having this suicidal conversation. You can't go there, not even with your mage partner." He paused and I could hear him yawning. "She's bad news. I was going to send Beck in after her. She's his kind of target."

"Did you locate her? Where did she go?"

There was a slight delay before he answered. "I did. She's at the Hellfire."

"Shit." The Hellfire was the worst place she could be.

"Told you I was sending in Beck. No one goes in there, but I'm guessing you aren't going to listen to me."

"Thanks, Ken. Can you call Beck off of Monty?"

"Once you bring in the mage you claim is responsible, the Council will call him off. Until then he's your nightmare. Oh, and he didn't appreciate the whole 'mummy' thing your mage did to him."

"I'll keep that in mind the next time I see him."

"Your funeral," he said and yawned again. "Don't call me again—ever."

The call disconnected. I walked to the Goat parked outside and unlocked it. Peaches stood next to me as I thought about the Hellfire. If The Den was the premier meeting place for Werewolves, the Hellfire was the place to be seen if you used magic in this city. It was also a deathtrap.

The old Hellfire was a BDSM club that had been shut down several times over the decades. The new Hellfire kept much of the décor and theme, but faced no threat of closure. Several wealthy backers made sure of that. Mages liked their kink, it seemed.

I made another call. "Ramirez, I need to get into the Hellfire and out again alive, without causing a war. Can you help me with this?"

"No, I can't even be seen near that place without catching heat from the brass. That place is for wizards and magic-users. Last I checked the only thing magical about you was your ability to wreak destruction on my city." He gave a heavy sigh. "Besides, I couldn't go even if I wanted to. We've had three more Werewolf incidents spread out over the city. I don't even want to think about what will happen when we get to the full moon."

"The full moon," I whispered, the realization hitting me. "How soon is the full moon?"

"Five days. We have five days to find out what's making them go crazy before we have a rabid Werewolf epidemic in the city. What's in the Hellfire?"

"I need to speak to a specific mage and she's in there." I said as I rubbed Peaches' head. "I can probably bypass the door, but then it'll get messy."

"NYTF and Hellfire have an unspoken *understanding*. They keep the magic under wraps, away from the general population, and we don't poke the hornet's nest. Did this mage break any laws?"

"No. I need her help, but I don't think she'll be cooperative, or happy to see me."

"And you're going to try and convince her to help you? More importantly, can you do this without destroying the building? Considering it's a landmark and in a sensitive area?"

"Monty is in Haven," I said quietly. "I have two days to get help from this mage or he's in trouble. I'm running out of options."

"Shit, why didn't you say so? I can't go, but I can send you Lieutenant Cassandra. As long as this is just speaking to someone, she can flash the badge and get you in the door at least."

"I owe you one," I said with a sigh of relief.

"You owe me more than one, but who's keeping track?" He yelled Cassandra's name before coming back on the line.. "When are you going?"

I opened the door for Peaches and we both got in. "Now."

"Done." Ramirez paused. "Is he okay? Was it because of what happened at The Den?"

"I don't know, but I'll keep you posted," I said as I started the engine. "Tell her to meet me at City Hall."

"Be careful down there," he said and hung up.

The Hellfire was located in the abandoned City Hall station under the current one. I headed that way.

TWENTY-TWO

The sun crept over the city as I sped downtown on 1st Avenue.

<I could eat something. A cow or two. Are we going to the place?>

I swerved but managed to regain control of the Goat, avoiding mounting the sidewalk and colliding with the few pedestrians who were already out at this early hour.

"A little warning would be good if you're going to be talking into my brain." I glanced into the back seat. Peaches stared at me through the rear-view mirror. "Is that really your voice?"

<I don't know, I've never heard myself. What do I sound like?>

"Vinnie Jones or a less-refined Monty," I said, aware of the fact that I was talking to my dog. "How are you doing this?"

<I stick my legs out and take up all the space. It feels good.>

"Not your sprawl. How are you speaking to me?" I made a turn to get on 2nd Avenue. "When did you start?"

<I've always spoken to you. But you never responded before now. I figured you just had poor hearing due to your silly excuse for ears. Do those things even work?>

I shot him another glance as we pulled up to the deli. "Yes, they work, but I don't think that's how we're talking." I got out of the Goat and opened the backdoor. "You coming?"

<The place!>

He bounded out of the car and kept pace with me as we headed to the entrance. We walked in, and the runes on the doorframe shimmered as we passed them. The old man sitting at the table in the corner looked up and motioned for us to join him. It was easy to confuse him with an elderly scholar. Who said Death didn't have a sense of humor?

It was before seven in the morning and the place was packed with patrons. This table was only ever occupied by the old man I knew as Ezra—except this time, he had a guest. Dressed in black, she sat opposite him with her back to me as I approached. She turned to glance my way with an expression of mild curiosity. Her pale face gave off a subtle glow. Well, half of it did. The other half was blue-black. She resembled the Valkyries I had met in Hades' building.

The little voice in my head pulled out a megaphone and promptly told me to turn around and run away. At another table directly across from them sat what I recognized as a Valkyrie and another large man. I looked around the deli and realized there were Valkyries seated in every corner of the place.

I pulled out a chair and greeted them both before I sat. I gave Ezra a short nod, which he returned. "Good morning, Ezra," I said and then gave the woman a short bow. If she was sitting with Ezra, there was a good chance she was important, or lethal. Probably both. Monty would want me to show some manners before pissing her off.

Ezra was dressed in his regular white shirt with black pants and a black vest. His rune-covered yarmulke gave off a faint violet glow, and he was poring over a thick book as usual. He closed it as I sat.

"This is Hel," he said with a gesture to the woman. "She won't be staying long."

She gave a brief nod at the mention of her name, and the blood flowed away from my face and rushed to my feet. "A pleasure," she said while staring at me with colorless eyes.

"Seems she has some work to see to." He gave her a look I couldn't decipher.

She gave me the onceover. "So this is Kali's chosen? Somehow I thought he would be more—robust."

"I only do 'robust' on the weekends. The rest of the week I do lean and mean." My heart did its best Savion Glover interpretation and tried to tap dance out of my chest. If I remembered correctly, Hel was the Norse equivalent to Hades, only with a mean streak and pain.

She gave me a long, hard stare, and then burst out laughing.

"I like him. I can see what Hades sees in him," she said as she looked down at Peaches. She held out a hand, but he didn't approach her. She smiled and nodded. "Your bond is strong. He reminds me of my brother, Fenrir, only smaller."

<I don't like her smell. Can I bite her?>

I put on my best poker face and didn't answer him. Her 'brother' was a monstrous wolf that went around chomping on gods. I didn't feel the need to point this out to her. I was getting a strong lethal-vibe from her, so I opted for tact. Monty would've been proud.

"Thank you for the comparison, Lady Hel. Peaches is a good dog," I said, rubbing his ears. "Fearsome in battle and in the devouring of pastrami."

"Peaches?" she said with a chuckle and looked at Ezra. He nodded, and she laughed again before growing serious. "Sadly, I can't stay. I have pressing matters to attend to. Your presence here means I no longer have to send Cathain after you."

"After me? Why would you send anyone after me?" I wondered how far I could get before one of the Valkyries stomped me.

Hel smiled at me. It was a killer's smile. The one you got right before your life was ripped apart, and your broken, lifeless body is lying shattered on the ground. Also the half-blue glowing face was making it hard to think friendly thoughts.

"Hades petitioned me to deliver this token to you. He must hold you in high esteem."

She motioned with her hand, and the man sitting with the Valkyrie came to our table. He was easily six-and-a-half feet tall and built like a house. When you thought 'Viking' this was the image that came to mind.

"Thank you, Lady, but no token is necessary—" I started, but shut up immediately when she raised a hand.

"This is Cathain Grobjorn, brewer of the Odinforce," she said interrupting me. The way she said his name, it sounded like Kane Groban, with a bunch of r's sprinkled in for good measure. "He has something for you. You have tasted his brew once before and survived. Cathain, the flask."

Cathain put a hand over his chest and bowed. "Yes, Mistress," he said. He pulled out a silver flask covered in glowing skulls and handed it to me. I held it out away from me and unscrewed the cap. I brought it to my nose, took a sip, and nearly lost my mind—it was coffee. Not just coffee, but *the* coffee. I had smelled this caffeinated ambrosia in Hades's office. It was in the vial Corbel had given me on Roosevelt Island. This was super coffee on steroids.

"It's *the* coffee?" I was incredulous. "How can this be coffee? And it's hot?"

"No mortal can drink of this brew without facing a painful and sudden death," she said, looking at me and standing. All of the Valkyries situated around the deli stood simultaneously. "This is the Odinforce, drink of the Valkyries and the fallen of Valhalla. Do you understand?"

I didn't, but I nodded my head, still in shock. She had just given me a flask full of Valhalla Java. "I understand," I whispered, holding the flask with reverence. The skulls on the surface coruscated with blue energy. "But this gift is too precious."

"The flask refills every evening," Cathain said, touching my shoulder. "Do not drink more than a spoonful at any given time."

"What happens if I drink more?" I asked, because it was going to be tough to only drink a spoonful of coffee this good.

"Honestly, with you I don't know," he said with a mischievous smile. "Increased strength, vitality, alertness, spontaneous combustion—why don't you try it and let me know? In any case, keep it safe. This is no light thing she has given you."

Gods and their jokes. Twisted didn't begin to describe their sense of humor.

Hel turned to Ezra. "I will speak to the All-Father, but he will not be pleased."

"What do I care for his pleasure?" Ezra said and waved his hand. "His pleasure or lack of it is of no consequence to me. He must act. Remind him that even *he* will meet with me one day."

"Very well," she said with a nod, and disappeared along with Cathain and all the Valkyries in the deli. If anyone noticed, they gave no indication. Business continued as usual. If I weren't holding the flask in my hand, I would've thought I'd imagined the whole thing.

"Ezra, what the hell? Why did she—?"

He waved my question away. "Eh eh shush, you have more important things to be worried about than her. Put that away. You eat first, and then we talk. No good conversation ever came from an empty stomach. What are you eating?"

"I was thinking some eggs—scrambled, maybe some toast, with some fries, and beef sausage. Peaches will have the usual." I settled into the chair and put the flask in a pocket.

He signaled to one of the waiters, who came over immediately. "Pastrami and eggs for him"—he pointed at me—"and ten pounds of pastrami for the puppy, in his special bowl."

I didn't bother arguing. It wasn't an argument I could win. When Death orders your breakfast, you eat it.

<I like how he smells. He smells like home.>

"He also happens to be death, as in Death—capital D," I whispered to Peaches. "Make sure you eat all of your pastrami. Don't leave any behind."

Peaches gave me a look and cocked his head to one side.

<Are you sure the dragon didn't throw you through a window? 'Don't leave any behind'? Why would I leave any of that delicious meat behind?>

I was about to answer, when a waiter came out with a large titanium bowl full of steaming pastrami, and put it on the floor in front of Peaches. He smelled the bowl and proceeded to devour the meat. A few minutes later, my plate arrived and I followed Peaches' example.

"You're talking to your puppy?" Ezra asked with a knowing smile. "You can hear him now—good."

"How did you…? Never mind," I said and kept eating.

"Finish your food." He looked down and petted Peaches on the head. No one ever touched Peaches while he ate, it was a good way to lose an arm. "The puppy has the right idea."

"We can't stay long, Ezra. Monty is—"

"How is Tristan?"

I swallowed the last bite of my breakfast and then spoke quickly. "Not good. He's in Haven. A Negomancer hit him with an erasure spell, and unless I get help from another mage, he'll lose his ability to cast magic

"This spell he's dealing with—it's not an erasure," he said, tapping the side of his nose and pointing at me. "He's mistaken. Trust me, my nose knows."

"But he said—" I started, but fell silent under his quiet gaze. Ezra had a way of making you rethink your words without saying any.

Ezra looked at me and slowly shook his head. "This Negomancer has underestimated your friend. It was supposed to be an erasure, but Tristan is too strong."

"What is it, then? The orb Roxanne showed me— she told me the spell would take away his ability to cast."

"She is mistaken, as is your friend. Sometimes the best action is inaction."

I sighed. "You sound like Master Yat with this fortune-cookie-speak. Can you just say what you want to say plainly?"

He patted my hand and slapped my cheek—hard. "I just did, but you aren't paying attention. Tristan will need a focus to work through this. When you see the mage, tell her you need a focus of three woods. She will understand."

"Of course she will because *that* is totally clear," I said, exasperated. I could hear the frustration in my voice but kept it in check, remembering whom I was speaking with. Being immortal was not an excuse to piss off Death.

"It will be to her. You're worried, this I understand. Family is important." He stood slowly with a groan. "Some days these old bones make it hard to get around. Simon, you will have to do some difficult things in the next few days. Remember what's important and you will see this through."

He shuffled to the back of the deli with a wave, and disappeared.

TWENTY-THREE

I jumped into the Goat, opened the window for Peaches in the back, and raced downtown. I understood half of what Ezra told me. What stayed with me was the message I was supposed to give Quan. *Monty needs a focus of three woods.* I turned the words over in my head, and they still made no sense. I pulled up to the City Hall and parked the car. Our NYTF registration made sure it was never towed. With Monty's runes, whoever tried would probably regret it.

In front of the stairs leading into the government building stood Cassandra. From her expression, I could tell she wasn't happy about escorting me. She placed a hand on her holster when she saw Peaches bound up next to me.

<Why is she scared? Remind her I shared my seat with her. I won't bite. Unless I can. Can I bite her?>

"No biting the lieutenant," I said under my breath as we approached. "Good morning, Lieutenant. Did Ramirez explain what we're going to do?"

She took a step back, keeping her distance from Peaches.

"Strong," she said with a quick nod. "He said I'm just here to get you into this 'Hellfire Club.' Strictly meet and greet. You need to speak to someone. I get you inside to speak to them."

I nodded. "It's going to be a little more complicated than that, but that's the gist of it." I turned to walk to the rear of the large building. She followed me with a surprised look on her face.

"I thought you were going to City Hall?" she said, pointing to the building. "The station is downstairs."

"You're talking about the train station. We don't need a train. We need a mage. We need to go lower. Under the current station." We made our way to the black kiosk obscured by trees, which stood about one hundred feet behind the building.

In front of the kiosk stood a woman dressed in a skintight, black-and-white checkered costume. Her face was hidden behind a black mask. The mask was a combination of tragedy and comedy. She bowed with a flourish and twirled the pair of rune-covered tonfas she held when I approached. This was one of the Harlequin—protectors of the Hellfire.

She stood to one side of the large, rune-inscribed circle that rested at the top of the stairs. In order to get into the Hellfire you needed to step in that circle—no exceptions.

"I need to see him," I said as I stood at the edge of the circle. "Is he in?"

The Harlequin twirled one of her tonfas and pointed at the circle.

"Is there a circus in town I don't know about?" Cassandra asked as she looked at the Harlequin. "What is she pointing at?"

I had grown so used to seeing runes and magic that I had forgotten it was invisible to most humans. Still, as part of the NYTF, I expected her to have some sensitivity to magic.

"They need to come too. She's NYTF and he's with me." I pointed at Cassandra. "Show her your badge, but do it slowly."

Cassandra reached inside her jacket pocket and pulled out her badge, showing it to the Harlequin, who nodded and gestured to the teleportation circle. I stepped forward and motioned for Cassandra to stand next to me. Peaches padded over to my other side and I nodded.

The Harlequin slammed both tonfas into the ground, and the circle we stood in flared to life. A second later, we stood at the foot of a flight of stairs that led to a large brass door.

The arch above us read "City Hall" in white tiled letters. The area was brightly lit, with each light fixture holding three lamps. The station was an art deco masterpiece and one of the hidden gems of New York.

Directly above us, embedded into the ceiling, was a large blue circular skylight. On its surface, runes danced and changed shapes. At the foot of the stairs stood two Harlequins, with another matching pair beside the brass door and entrance to the club.

The next second, the nausea hit me, and my breakfast threatened to claw out of my stomach. I hated teleportation. It always had the effect of twisting my insides out. Peaches looked unbothered, but Cassandra was a little green as she leaned against the wall.

"What the hell was that?" she said, clutching her stomach. "Oh, my God, I feel sick."

"Give it a few seconds, it'll pass," I felt queasy myself and didn't dare to take the stairs yet. "It's an effect of the spatial displacement."

She shook her head and stepped away from the wall. "The what?"

"The teleportation messes with your insides, which is why you feel like someone tied your intestines into a knot. Takes getting used to."

"I don't ever want to get used to that. Is that it?" She pointed at the brass door, and I nodded. When I felt like my breakfast was safe and secure in my stomach, I took the steps slowly.

"Whatever you see in there, don't say—or more importantly, don't *do*—anything," I warned when we got to the door. "No one is in danger, and everything that's occurring is consensual."

"I wasn't raised on the moon, Strong," she said adjusting her holster. "There isn't much that can shock me at this age."

"Just remember what I said and don't overreact."

I bowed to the Harlequins at the door. They returned the bow and stood at attention. These women weren't window-dressing. According to Monty, the man I came to see handpicked and trained each one. The Harlequins were accomplished mages and could wield their runed tonfas with deadly efficiency. In other words, if you followed the rules, you left Hellfire alive; if you broke them, you didn't.

"I need to see him," I said at the door and then waited. If the symbol that appeared on the door was black, it meant we were denied. No questions asked, no excuses taken, no exceptions. If it was white, we were past the first of three gates.

"What are we waiting for?" Cassandra asked under her breath. "Do you have to make an appointment?"

The symbol on the door flared white, and the door slid away. I exhaled in relief. My "plan B" involved Monty-levels of destruction. We walked down a long, narrow, featureless hallway. At the end of it stood a woman with a crow on her shoulder, and I cursed under my breath.

The second gate was always a god. Sometimes you lucked out and got Eros, or any of the other obscure minor gods, like Philyra—goddess of paper and crafts, who once asked me to make an origami eagle that could fly.

Pantheons didn't matter in the second gate. Occasionally you would get a heavy-hitter, one of the big names. Then, sometimes, you would get the woman standing at the other end of the hallway. I didn't know how the Hellfire managed it, but I guessed the gods were bored and this brought them some measure of excitement.

"Who's that?" Cassandra whispered s she reached for her gun. I grabbed her hand and shook my head. She was reacting to the woman's presence. It took a few seconds before the lieutenant calmed down. Peaches stood by my side in ready mode but he didn't seem overly agitated.

We approached the woman and I bowed. The woman nodded at me and cocked her head to one side when she looked at Cassandra.

"Hello, Simon—who cannot be chosen," she said without taking her eyes off Cassandra. "It warms my cold heart to see you again."

"Hello, Morgan. The honor is truly mine. You look well."

"She is human and has no voice here. You will speak for the group, yes?" She dismissed Cassandra with a look and stared at me.

"Yes, I will speak for the group. Please ask your question." I tried to keep my voice from shaking. Meeting the Morrigan always filled me with dread. Even though I was immortal, and she reinforced it, she always said it as an invitation to find out if it was true.

She was the Celtic equivalent of the Valkyries except she had a few differences. The Morrigan chose the slain, but on occasion, she got her hands dirty and joined in the wars with her chosen. She also fell in love —and it usually ended badly for those warriors. Her question would be one of the hardest, which is why Monty made sure I studied her.

"My question is in three parts since your group is three," she said with a brief smile and pushed the crow off her shoulder. It vanished in a cloud of feathers. She was enjoying herself, which was never a good sign.

"I understand." I took a deep breath. If I failed any of the three parts, she could make any request and we would have to fulfill it—or suffer the consequences.

She raised a finger. "How many times did I appear to my beloved?" She raised another finger. "How did I choose him?" Another finger…"What was his name?"

I gave it some thought and silently thanked Monty for making me read the story of Cu Chulainn several times.

"Four times did you appear to him. You washed his clothes at the fjord. His name was Cu Chulainn," I said, making sure to answer the questions in the same order she asked them. A right answer out of sequence was still wrong.

She stared at me for a few seconds and then nodded. "Your group may pass, but before you go" —she crouched down to rub Peaches' ears, looking up at me —"*aire a thabhairt do maité, Peitseogach*. Remember what is important, immortal." She transformed into a crow and flapped down the hallway.

It was the second time I'd had heard those words.

Peaches gave a rumble in response and the crow disappeared. The wall where she'd stood disappeared too, and I let out the breath I had been holding. One more gate to go as we stepped into the next room.

TWENTY-FOUR

The third gate was the hardest, and I had only passed it last time with Monty's help. So this time, without him, we were screwed. It was always a magical question and my ability and memory for magic and runes was horrible, no matter what Monty said.

"We may have to improvise on this one, so get ready," I whispered to Cassandra and kept my hand close to Grim Whisper. Her encounter with the Morrigan had left her shell-shocked. She nodded her head, but I could tell she was having difficulty processing the events. I think the fieldwork was becoming a bit much for her already.

We stood in a large library. Every wall was covered with books and shelves. Spread out around the room were desks and tables with books stacked on them. In the center of the room floated a large blackboard. Around it stood four men and one woman.

All of them were dressed in white robes covered with silver runic brocade. They were magic-users, and from the looks of the robes, powerful ones. The woman was bald like Quan and I wondered if she was also a member of the White Phoenix. Unlike Quan, she had no tattoos on her face or head. She glided over to us.

"Hello, Simon. I am Syght. Welcome to the last gate." She handed me a silver stylus about a foot in length and then pointed at the board. "This one is simple. Please trace the rune for that which is the most important on the board."

I stepped up to the board and hesitated. Each gate corresponded to one of the three areas. The first, being body, scanned us for any malignant spells, casting or weapons. The second, mind, tested knowledge and its correct transmission. The third was spirit and revealed principles and ideals. The five mages represented the five senses. My answer provided the sixth or elevated sense required to pass the gate.

I couldn't just write "water" or "air," as those answers didn't reveal the spirit. Then there was the complication that I had to answer for the group, since Cassandra wasn't a magic-user. I had to factor in what she may consider most important and give as an answer. Peaches was easy, since his love of pastrami was second only to his protectiveness of me. I'm sure most of that was the bond we shared, but I felt that he genuinely liked me. Maybe it was a close tie with pastrami.

"I need a moment," I said and stepped over to where Cassandra and Peaches stood waiting.

"Please take your time." Syght waited by the board.

"What's the matter?" Cassandra asked. "Do you know the answer?"

"To what's most important? Yes," I said after a moment. "I know what's most important to me and to Peaches."

"I'm the mystery?" She looked at the blackboard. "And if you get this one wrong?"

"I'm pretty sure we get dumped outside and told not to return for a while," I lied, keeping my voice even as I tapped the stylus against my other hand. "What's most important to you?"

I really hoped Cassandra had a good answer. If she said something like "staying alive," I would go with my answer and hope for the best. I knew if we failed at this gate, the consequence was severe. An incorrect answer of the spirit meant corruption, and they dealt with that harshly—usually extermination. No pressure.

"My dad," she said after a pause. "He's the reason I'm in the NYTF in the first place. I'm always trying to impress him. My whole life I've just wanted to hear him say "I'm proud of you" just once."

I nodded my head. "Thanks, that's a good answer."

It *was* a good answer. I stepped back to the board and Syght looked at me expectantly. "Are you ready to continue?"

"Yes, I am," I coughed to regain my voice. For a second, I preferred standing in front of the Morrigan.

"As the voice for your group, do you accept the terms of failure?" she asked, her voice grim. Her eyes began to glow violet as she placed a hand on the board, making it glow the same color.

"If I fail, can I take on the failure alone, as the voice of the group?"

She shook her head slowly. "No, I'm sorry. Each will share in the consequence of the failure if incorrect. You speak for all three. Do you need more time?"

They were going to have a hard time trying to kill

me, but Cassandra wasn't immortal. I figured Peaches, considering his pedigree, was indestructible, and probably measured his dog years in centuries. This was a huge risk if I was wrong. I opened my coat and made sure I had easy access to Grim Whisper and Ebonsoul. If this went south, we weren't going down easy.

I placed the stylus on the board and began to trace one of the few runes I did know. Monty had tried to get me to study the basic Elder Futhark marks as my ability to see runic castings became clearer. I had given him a migraine after ten minutes and he threatened to incinerate me after twenty. I stopped studying them after that, but I did remember this rune because of what it meant.

I traced a diamond with the bottom two legs extended and crossing each other. Its name was Othala. It was easy to remember because it looked like the top of the endless knot mark on the back of my left hand.

Syght held her hand outstretched and I gave her the stylus. The rune glowed violet like her eyes as the five of them turned the board away from me and examined my answer.

I walked back to Peaches and Cassandra with my hand resting on my holster.

"Get ready to move if they decide I'm wrong," I whispered under my breath and loosened Grim Whisper in its holster.

Cassandra adjusted her holster as well. "Will regular bullets work on these guys?"

"Probably not, but shoot them anyway and give me time to get close. My blade will work where bullets won't."

She nodded and bladed her body slightly. Her
training showed and she seemed to overcome the
earlier shock. Either that or she was anxious to shoot
something, which still worked out in our favor as long
as she didn't shoot me or Peaches.

The mages fanned out as Syght approached. It didn't
look good and I let my hand rest on Grim Whisper as
she got closer. She looked down at my hand and
outstretched her arms. Orbs of white energy spun in
her hands.

"If you draw your weapon, I will be forced to hurt
you and kill your friends. Is this the outcome you
desire?" she said quietly. "Would you like to hear our
determination before we try to kill each other? Or
should we just unleash havoc and see who survives?"

I took my hand off Grim Whisper, and the orbs in
her hands disappeared in response.

"I won't let you hurt them," I said, my voice holding
the promise of violence. "If you touch them, you *will*
have to kill me, and that won't be easy."

"Your answer was…unique, but based on your
behavior, quite adequate. You may pass the third gate.
Erik is waiting for you."

A rune flared on the door at the other end of the
library as she pointed to it. For a second it was too
surreal, and then I realized the point of my visit. I
bowed to Syght and the other four mages before
crossing the floor and heading for the door.

"Thank you," I said with a sigh of relief. "I'm really
glad we held off on that unleashing-havoc thing."

She nodded at me but held up her hand. "A word
about your answer, Simon, before you enter and see

him."

I stopped walking and turned to face her. "Was something wrong with my answer?" I felt my stomach drop and my heart constrict at her words.

"Your answer was correct for your group. It isn't the only correct answer. Your response is your greatest strength and your most debilitating weakness. Tread carefully."

"I will, thank you again," I said and then headed for the door with Peaches and Cassandra next to me.

"What was your answer?" Cassandra asked as we headed to the entrance.

"You're here because of your father. Peaches is here because of me, and I'm here because of Monty. The only answer that made sense was...family. That's what's most important. That's what I wrote on the board."

I took hold of the handle and opened the door.

TWENTY-FIVE

We stepped into another teleportation circle as we crossed the threshold with a flash of bright light. Another wave of nausea hit me, but milder this time. That meant the distance we traveled was shorter.

We entered a large open floor area that could only be described as a dungeon. I stood still for a few seconds until the nausea passed and then I looked around. There were various stations located throughout the floor. Most of them were implements of pain and torture. Others were being used for restraint. Men and women occupied all of them equally. A walk through Hellfire was a crash course through the exotic world of pain as pleasure. It wasn't my world, though I wondered if what I had with Michiko didn't make me a masochist of sorts.

I nudged the "unshockable" Cassandra, who stood transfixed at the scene.

"Is that...is that even legal? Isn't she in pain?" She was pointing at one of the stations where a woman was being held down by runed straps of leather that simultaneously shocked and constricted her body.

"Judging from her squeals of delight, I would say no. As for legal, only two laws exist in this place: consent is paramount, and no magic-use to harm or injure. After that, anything goes. Close your mouth. I wouldn't want you to appear shocked."

She quickly shut her mouth as we walked across the floor. A few of the mages invited her to join them and laughed when she blushed and gave them the stink-eye for an answer.

All of the mages in the club knew of Michiko. Her reputation was respected and feared in every supernatural community. It also meant that all I got was the cold shoulder as we made our way to the large table situated on a raised dais at the far end of the room. No one wanted to piss her off. Everyone seemed to know about the date.

Erik sat there flanked by his inner circle of mages. If the Last Supper had been held in a BDSM club full of mages, it would look something like the image that welcomed me as I climbed the stairs of the dais.

"Hello, Erik," I said as he unlatched his lips from the

mage sitting next to him. She purred in feigned anger and shot me a dirty look. "I need a moment of your time."

"Simon," he said, looking in my direction. "When did you arrive? Why didn't you call me? I could have spared you the gates."

It was all pretense. No one avoided the gates—ever. He knew where I was the moment I spoke to the Harlequin standing behind City Hall. No one entered Hellfire without his knowledge. As far as mages went, Monty once told me Erik was on par with any of the Golden Circle mages. He was also the only sitting mage representative on the Dark Council. It meant he wielded a considerable amount of power and influence.

When I asked Monty who was more powerful between them, he only said it wasn't a fight he enjoyed thinking about. In Monty-speak, it meant he had considered it, planned it out, and worked out most if not all of the probable outcomes.

Erik stood abruptly and pushed his chair back with a flourish. "Follow me, please," he said as he walked off the dais. "I have just the place for us. A little more intimate."

He was dressed in a dark suit, which mages seemed to favor, with a silver tinged shirt. His long legs crossed the distance to the door by the table in several strides. We caught up with him as he placed his hand on the wall beside the door. Runes flared to life and the door opened into a spacious office. Two Harlequins bookended his desk.

He sat down in an oversized chair and waited as one of the Harlequins poured him a clear drink from a waiting decanter and then returned to her station. The office, though large, felt inviting. Bookshelves filled with books covered every wall. I looked around, admiring the collection.

"There's this new invention called an e-book. You might've heard of it. Save yourself some much needed space."

"I must confess I'm a bit of a bibliophile. Nothing smells or feels quite the same as a four-hundred-year-old book," he said, placing his feet on the desk. "Besides, physical books are *magic*. Now, how can I help you?"

I sat down as he sipped his drink. "I need to see Quan."

"Who?"

"Don't bullshit me, Erik. This is important and I know she's here."

"Obviously, or else you wouldn't be sitting here with such lovely company." He looked over at Cassandra. "And your name is?"

"Lieutenant," she said and flashed him her NYTF badge.

"Ooh, an official visit," he said with a chuckle. "She sounds like she likes it rough. Do you like it rough, Lieutenant?"

Cassandra, to her credit, didn't shoot him. She took a step forward and the Harlequins shifted positions faster than I could track. Both of them stood in front of Cassandra in a defensive stance with their tonfas ready. Cassandra froze in place and took a small step back. The Harlequins relaxed their stance slightly.

I unholstered Grim Whisper, unsheathed Ebonsoul

slowly, and placed them both on his desk. "I need to speak to Quan—now," I said, urgency creeping into my voice as I stood. I stepped away from the desk and my weapons.

He remained silent as he looked down at my weapons. He steepled his fingers and brought them to his lips.

"The Hellfire is a designated neutral location. No one brings violence into my home. No one," he said after a moment.

"Tell that to the men and women strapped and tied down outside," Cassandra muttered under her breath.

"My dear, that's not violence, that's exquisite torture. Like our esteemed Marquis said—sex without pain is like food without taste, and I do enjoy my meals full of taste," He slowly licked his lips.

"I'm fasting for the foreseeable future," Cassandra said as she inched closer to the door. "In fact I may never eat again after meeting you."

Erik laughed and then grew serious. He fixed me with his gaze and sighed.

"I'll take you to Quan. But if you or that animal you call a dog—"

"Peaches. His name is Peaches and he's just a puppy." I rubbed his head. "He has a name."

He stood up. "If you do anything to violate the neutrality of this place, I will end you, Simon, and your little beast of a dog too. Come with me. You can get these back *if* you leave." He waved his hands over my weapons and they vanished from the top of the desk.

"Don't you mean *when* I leave?" I asked as we headed to another door in his office.

Erik gave me a sidelong glance. "I heard what happened to the new neutral location. Your track record speaks for itself. I meant '*if*.'"

"Did you know that it was Quan who trashed The Randy Rump? She took out three Council vampires in as many seconds. I was there when it happened—on neutral ground." Now I was angry. "I don't see why you are protecting her here."

"Because I choose to. I don't owe you an explanation, Simon. Life is unfair. I'd get used to it if I were you."

"You know, mages can really suck sometimes," I said as I threw my hands up, frustrated.

"You have no idea," he said with a smile. "Anyway, after Tristan refused to turn himself in, they sent the Negomancer."

"Did you have something to do with the decision to send Beck after Monty?" I asked as he opened the door. "Were you part of that?"

He shrugged. "No. Out of the five Council heads, only two dissented. I thought it was a bad idea letting Beck loose on the streets of New York. He's slightly deranged. Michiko probably wanted to keep your friend alive. The others really don't like you two."

I made a mental note as we walked through the door into an outdoor Zen garden. I did a double-take and looked back into his office. I didn't feel nauseated, but we were outside and, from the looks of the iconic volcano in the distance, we were in Japan.

"How are we in Japan without my stomach doing somersaults?"

"We are and we aren't," he said and pointing back to

the office door. "That anchor, the Hellfire, keeps us fixed in one place but the spell I cast acts as a time and spatial displacer."

The glazed look in my eyes must have clued him in to the fact that he was speaking *mage* and had lost me.

"Excuse me, what?" Cassandra said, looking around in amazement. "We're in Japan? Is that Mt. Fuji?"

"The Hellfire acts like an anchor. The spell allows us to travel anywhere. It only works in the Hellfire and it cost a fortune in runes and money to pull off. Better?"

I nodded and looked across the garden. In the distance sat Quan.

"Can I go talk to her?" I wasn't sure if there was an etiquette I needed to follow.

"Leave your friends here. The door will remain active until you walk through. This" —he stretched out an arm and gestured around us—"is still part of the Hellfire. Don't piss her off and don't destroy anything," he said before he vanished.

"Where did he go? What are we doing in Japan?" Cassandra asked, clearly agitated. "What the hell?"

"Take a breath and calm down. He went back to the club. He was just showing off. If I had to guess, I would say this is a tethered pocket dimension connected to the Hellfire." I peered around, feeling as amazed as she looked. "I'm not sure. For all I know we could actually be in Japan."

She waved me away. "You're making about as much sense as the creepy horny mage did. Let's do what we came here to do. The sooner you're done the sooner we get back."

"Wait here, I'll go talk to her," I said to them both.

*<This looks like a good place to dig. Can I dig a small hole?
>*

"No digging or making any holes," I said aloud before I realized my mistake. "I mean, don't disturb the stones."

The expression on Cassandra's face only reinforced that I was going to have to learn how to communicate with him silently.

"What? I know what a Zen garden is, Simon," Cassandra said, confused. "No one is going to go digging holes. Go talk to her."

Peaches gave me a grunt and sat on his haunches as Cassandra settled on the bench. She really couldn't have gotten any further away from Peaches if she tried.

TWENTY-SIX

Quan sat with her eyes closed as I approached.

"Hello, Simon. Why are you here without Tris?" She hadn't moved an inch or opened her eyes.

"I need—I mean, Monty seriously needs help. He's going through something. I thought it was an erasure but Ezra says it's not. He said you need to give him a focus of three woods, whatever that is. Roxanne said she needed a powerful mage, and you were the only one that came to mind."

She opened her eyes slowly and looked at me.

"I don't know any Ezra. A focus of three woods is nearly impossible to make." She looked at me and narrowed her eyes. "What's this about? Who told you about the focus?"

I shook my head. "You wouldn't believe me if I told you. I think Beck—a Negomancer—cast an erasure on Monty. Now it's out of control and he may lose his casting ability. That's why I'm here."

"An erasure? On Tristan? You do know he's a battle mage?"

I nodded. "But Roxanne showed me this orb. She said it represented—"

"Is she a mage?"

"No, but she's close to him. The orb she showed me had this black ring around it and—"

"Unless she's a mage, she can't show you an accurate representation of Tristan's energy," she said, cutting me off again. "It doesn't matter if she's *close*, she's mistaken."

"Then what did she show me? His energy was surrounded by blackness."

"A battle mage is the closest thing to a weapon of last resort any sect possesses. They are powerful, dangerous, ill-tempered mages no one wants to cross. This Roxanne showed you her fear."

"That description sounds like Monty," I muttered. "But even he thinks it's an erasure."

"Battle mages are also shielded from an early age against any kind of Negomancy. A Negomancer, even a powerful one with time to prepare, would only irritate a mage at Tristan's level. This is something else that is acting like an erasure."

"Is he going dark? Is that what you mean?"

She remained silent for a few seconds, which wasn't

encouraging. Her eyes went out of focus as she gazed off into the distance. She snapped back suddenly and looked at me. "If Tristan Montague went dark, I would be forced to kill him," she whispered. "But this is a power shift. He's increasing in power—he just doesn't recognize what's happening to him. He's never seen a power shift at his level. It doesn't happen too often."

"That's why I'm here. If it's not an erasure, I— Monty—needs the help of another mage. Roxanne thinks it's an erasure, but she doesn't know for certain."

"If you needed a mage, why didn't you solicit Erik?" she said, pointing at the door back to Hellfire. "He is a powerful and accomplished mage and sits on your Dark Council."

"Because he acts like a hormonal teenager who just discovered sex." I paused when the real reason hit me. "I don't trust Erik or the Dark Council."

She shook her head slowly and settled back into her seated pose, closing her eyes. "I'm busy trying to prevent an apocalypse. I'm sorry, I can't. I can't help Tristan. We have too much history. Find another mage. My focus and priority is stopping the madness Davros is unleashing. There are other mages in the club."

"You sensed it, didn't you? In the shop? When you first saw Monty I remember you said he needed to get ready for the shift."

"You need to leave," she said keeping her eyes closed. "Another mage can help him—any mage but me. Trust me, he won't want my help."

I felt a wave of anger wash over me and quickly struggled to keep it in check. She sure didn't look very busy sitting in the middle of a Zen garden in some pocket dimension with her eyes closed, but I couldn't afford to piss her off. Monty needed her help, so I tried a different strategy—ego bruising.

My experience with magic-users was that most of them were insecure, with thin skin. If you approached them the right way, it didn't take much to push their buttons and set them off. The problem with this theory was that they were *magic-users*. They wielded insane amounts of lethal energy and if you got them angry, they directed that energy at *you*.

So far, only Monty had disproven this theory. He didn't need to be provoked to unleash ungodly energy at me. It was his default setting. I had a feeling Quan was the same way.

"You're going to need help," I whispered as I sat on the stones in front of her. "Davros isn't alone."

"The Werewolves being turned are no threat to me. If they stand in my way, I'll eliminate them. The Permutation isn't complete."

"I wasn't talking about the Werewolves. Davros has real help—the kind of help you won't be able to face alone," I said, picking up a stone and tossing it to one side. "It's the kind of help that makes mages like you *run*."

She cocked her head to the side where I had thrown the stone. "Davros is working alone. No one would help a madman like him."

"You said he stole the Phoenix Tail from your group, which means your security basically sucks," I stated with a shrug. "How did he get the drake's blood? Did you leave that lying around with the Tail? Isn't drake's blood rare? I can't imagine dragons going around offering blood to humans—especially considering what it can do."

She opened her eyes and glared at me. It was a glare worthy of three Eastwoods on my glare-scale. From the flexing of her jaw and the shift in her body language, I could tell I'd hit the right buttons. Like I said—insane energy and power…in thin skin. She flexed her fingers which reminded me of Monty.

"Do you usually find yourself on the verge of annihilation from the words that escape your mouth? Or are you suicidal?"

"It's a gift," I said with a slight nod. "So, how did Davros get the blood?"

"It's rare, but it's possible the Golden Circle had some in their archive. He could have stolen it from there."

I shook my head. "Doubt it. Monty told me about the Sanctuary. At least *they* take their security seriously, unlike the White Phoenix."

"Our artifacts are contained securely. Davros betrayed us." She scowled, the muscles in her jaw working furiously as she spoke.

"Golden Circle artifacts are sealed away so tight you'd need the equivalent of a magical nuke to even get near their vaults. No way Davros stole it from them. Hey, here's a thought, maybe you should have your security person talk to the Golden Circle? Get some pointers on how to keep world-ending artifacts out of the hands of mages who've lost their minds?"

"You need to cease your prattle before I hit you with something world-ending," she said, forming an orb of air in her hand.

"He has a dragon helping him. Davros isn't working alone." I made to stand, but she placed a hand on my arm, effectively holding me in place.

"What did you say?" The orb in her hand evaporated. "He has a what?"

"Her name is Slif and she should be back in a few days," I said and slid back as she stood suddenly. "You met her at The Randy Rump."

"That woman was no dragon," she said with a mixture of fear and urgency in her voice "At best, she was a drake and she certainly wasn't Slif. I've met Slif and that wasn't her."

I nodded quickly. "The innocent drake look was an illusion—a good one. You know Slif?"

"I do. I don't understand how you faced her and survived. How is this possible? You possess no power except possibly the power to infuriate."

"Monty cast a void vortex around her and shipped her to Siberia. He said she would be back in few days."

"He cast a *void vortex*? In the center of a populated city?"

"Yes, he said Slif was too powerful to face." I finally got to my feet as she began walking to the doorway that anchored us to Hellfire. I motioned for Cassandra and Peaches to follow us.

"Has he gone bloody daft? The Golden Circle will be after him for sure now," she muttered to herself before turning suddenly to face me. "Where is he? Where is that damn fool?"

"Don't know if I want to share that with you now, you seem a bit on the angry magey side," I said, holding my hands up in surrender. "Maybe after you calm down or have a 'spot of tea.' Doesn't that usually do the trick?"

"So help me, Simon" —she flexed her hands as she spoke—"if you don't tell me where he is right this moment, I will violate the neutral sanctity of this place and reduce you to ashes," she whispered, her voice laced with grim determination.

I figured by that point I had pushed every button I needed to push. "He's in Haven. It's a medical—" I started.

"I know what it is and where. I have sensed Davros somewhere north of the city, but we need to go see Tristan now."

TWENTY-SEVEN

"I thought I told you *not* to piss her off?" Erik said as we walked through the club, following Quan. "What part of that sentence was unclear?"

"The part where if I don't get her to help me, Monty loses his ability to cast," I shot back, trying to keep up with Quan. "What's the big deal? She's leaving and your club is intact. I call that a win-win."

"She is setting off *all* the security measures," he said, exasperated as he swept his arm around the club. "She's bleeding off so much power the runic defenses think we're under attack and locking the place down,"

I followed his arm and saw runes flaring all around us. Doors were slamming shut with huge iron bars falling into place to secure them. In some locations steel gates descended, cutting off entire areas.

"Just reset them?" I offered apologetically.

"Why do you think I had her in a separate dimension *away* from the club?" he hissed. "To prevent *this*. Don't you know who she is?"

I gave him a blank stare. "Quan from the White Phoenix?"

"Your astounding ignorance staggers the imagination, Simon," He pinched the bridge of his nose. "She is the daughter of Master Toh—the leader of the White Phoenix. Simply put, the only mage who would consider going up against her would be Tristan, and I don't know who would win that fight."

I looked at Quan again. I knew she was powerful after what she did at the Rump, I just didn't think she was *that* powerful. I made a mental note not to push any of her buttons in the future. Erik grabbed me by the arm and pulled me to a sudden stop.

"What the—?"

All around us, runic circles materialized on the floors and walls. Each one glowed bright red or deep orange. The circles gave off a strange energy signature that made even Peaches whine in discomfort.

"You don't want to step in one of those," he said directing us away from them.

"What are those?" I pointed to one as we walked by, careful to avoid stepping in or on it. "They feel unfriendly."

He looked at the rune-filled circles. "I'm surprised you can see them. They're called oblivion circles. This is going to take days to disable and reset, Simon. You must allow me to express my heartfelt thanks one day."

"Erik, I'm sorry, I didn't think she'd react this way. I just told her about the dragon and she lost it."

He grabbed my shoulder. "Dragon? What dragon?" *What dragon?*

"Did you say dragon?" Cassandra asked. I waved her question away while nodding. "As in fire-breathing snake-like creature?"

"There's one due in the city in a few days. Monty sent her on a Russian holiday but she's going to come back and she won't be pleased."

"Why didn't you say something about this dragon earlier?" Erik said and made a gesture. Several of the oblivion circles blocking our path disappeared. "Do you realize how dangerous this is? A dragon in the city will cause massive destruction and death."

"You didn't ask me, and I'm here to get Monty help so we can deal with a mage who's being helped by this dragon. This is where the Werewolf turnings are coming from."

Erik pulled out his phone. "Shit. I have to call the Council. We aren't prepared for a dragon."

"I don't think anyone is, really. Monty barely got her trapped in time."

"Trapped? How did he trap her? Tell me he didn't use a void vortex or something equally insane. Please say it was a containment field of some kind and then he displaced it."

"I won't say he didn't use a void vortex," I started, but decided against finishing when he narrowed his eyes at me. We caught up to Quan, who stood by the large brass door. Erik placed a hand by the frame, causing runes to flare to life, and the door swung open.

"He damn well used a bloody vortex," Quan said as she opened the door stepped into a teleportation circle. "Call your Council and get them ready. I'll deal with Tristan if the Golden Circle hasn't negated him by now. Hurry up, Simon."

The next moment, she was gone. I turned to Erik.

"What? Negated? Why would they negate him?" I asked, confused, as we stepped out of the club. "He got a dragon out of the city. They should be thanking him."

"He used a forbidden spell to dispatch the dragon," Erik said and placed his hand by the door again. "The Golden Circle will view that as a crime and want to make an example out of him. Don't come back here unless invited."

"Weapons?" I said, looking at him. "You can return them now."

He waved his hand in the air and my weapons materialized, hovering in front of me. "Actually, just don't come back," he said as I grabbed them.

The door slammed shut in my face and Cassandra jumped next to me. I took a step back into the circle behind us and we appeared in front of the kiosk outside, behind City Hall. The Harlequin at the top of the stairs gave me a short bow, which I returned. Quan stood next to the Goat.

"I'm assuming this is your car judging from the runes?" she asked, looking closely at the surface of the car.

I placed my hand on the handle and unlocked the car to clangs and an orange wave of energy. "Monty wanted to make sure we were safe. This car took a blast from a dragon without damage."

"He included a Ziller Effect? How did Tristan manage that? Getting that effect to protect anything larger than an amulet has melted the brain of several mages—quite literally."

"He tried explaining this Ziller thing to me and almost melted *my* brain. All I know is that it prevented Slif from flame-broiling me."

She shook her head in wonder and stepped around the passenger side. "This car is virtually indestructible to magic-based attacks."

I opened the door and Peaches bounded into the back seat, followed by a wary Cassandra. Quan slid next to me into the passenger seat as I started the car. She took a deep breath and closed her eyes. After a few seconds, she opened them and looked around the interior.

"The rune-work on this vehicle is extensive. What exactly does Tristan expect to encounter while driving around this city? What kind of enemies *do* you have?"

"Lately it's just been dragons." I pulled away, headed uptown. "But we get the occasional Werewolf pack or angry god."

She turned and gave me a look of disapproval. "God? This is no time for jokes, Simon."

"I know," I said, serious, and stepped on the gas. The sun was setting and I wanted to get to Haven before Ken sent Beck after Quan.

TWENTY-EIGHT

I had called Roxanne ahead of our arrival and she directed us to the Detention Center. She met us outside as I pulled up.

"Why are we at the DC?" I asked as I got out of the car.

Roxanne pulled out a keycard and placed it and against the card reader by the door. "It's Monty. Whatever he's dealing with isn't an erasure. We had to 'contain' him. We couldn't do it in the medical wing." She pulled the door open and motioned for us to go in.

"Obviously," Quan said, crossing her arms. "Any mage could see that."

"And this is?" Roxanne asked, looking at me.

"You needed a powerful mage, I got you a powerful mage," I gestured to Quan. "This is Quan of the White Phoenix."

Quan gave her a short nod and proceeded to walk past her and into the building. "Tristan is below us. We need to get to him now."

"How do you know where he is?" Roxanne said as she tried to keep up with Quan. "Who are you again? He never mentioned knowing a Quan."

"What do you mean 'contain'?" I asked as we approached the elevators. "Doesn't the medical wing have a containment unit?"

"We're going to sub-level four," she said as we entered the elevator and she placed the card against the panel. "Our containment unit wasn't strong enough.

He burned through eight levels of defensive layers before we could hold him down. Eight levels in a matter of seconds."

"What does that mean?" I asked, feeling nervous. "Has he turned into some mage monster?"

Quan and Roxanne regarded me with the 'I can't believe you just said that' look. So I just looked at Peaches and rubbed his head.

<*They say a bite is worth a thousand words. Want me to bite them?*>

I suppressed a chuckle. "I think you have that one confused, boy," I said under my breath and rubbed his ears. "No biting."

"You have access to sub-level four?" Cassandra asked, surprised. "I thought only NYTF top-level clearance knew about this place?"

"I *thought* Ramirez shut this place down after they discovered it was a black site?" I remembered the last time I was here.

"They did," Cassandra said as the elevator stopped moving. "He made sure it was decommissioned for NYTF use. I didn't know it was still being used." The doors remained closed until Roxanne placed a thumb on the panel. A bright light scanned her finger. That was new.

"Sub-level four is now a part of the Detention Center and is overseen by the Haven staff," Roxanne said, inserting a key into the panel. "This level is meant to house the most dangerous magic-users. We have oversight now and regular visits from NYTF inspectors."

"Who's being housed here now?" I asked as the door

opened.

"Only Tristan is on this level right now," she said as she stepped out of the elevator and onto the floor. "No other magic-user in our Detention Center warrants this kind of containment." The floor right outside the elevator was covered in runes, which flared bright yellow as we stepped on them. In fact, the entire floor leading to all of the cells was inscribed with runes.

The floor plan was unchanged. The level was a large rectangle with three massive cell doors in each of the four sides. A right turn at the end of the hallway put us facing another row of cells. Spotlights had been added, illuminating the center of each of the sides.

Quan looked down at the floor. "Devastation runes? Impressive," she said with admiration.

"Along with a few others," Roxanne said, continuing to walk down the hallway. "No one is escaping this level."

I knew which cell she was leading us to and it made perfect sense. How do you contain a mage whose power is increasing? You place him in a cell designed to hold a being of great power. Monty was in Charon's old cell.

TWENTY-NINE

"You know what is happening to Tristan?" Roxanne asked as we approached the door of his cell. "Can you explain it?"

Quan studied the runes on the door and stiffened. "No. I can't. Can you explain the intricacies of sorcery to me?"

"I can explain theory—wait, how did you know I was a sorceress?"

"Who placed these runes on the door?" Quan said, her voice tight with anger. "They are only delaying the process."

"They were part of the design of the room," Roxanne snapped back, clearly upset. "This cell was created to hold beings of great power. It was the only place we could put him. I don't care for your tone. I'm doing everything in my power to help Tristan and—"

"It's not enough," Quan whispered. She stepped close to the door and closed her eyes. "He isn't going through an erasure, but the runes in this cell are preventing the power shift. He's in stasis. I need to go inside."

"You can't," Roxanne said, and Quan opened her eyes, leveling her gaze at her. Roxanne put her hands up. "It's not that I won't let you, we can't open the door. It's sealed from the inside."

"Do you have an archive here?" Quan asked with urgency.

"A what?" Roxanne answered confused. "Our records are stored digitally. Why would you need to see our records?"

"Not records—a storehouse where you keep magical supplies. A vault?"

"Oh, yes, we do in the medical wing. We have the most extensive—"

"I need runed wood," Quan said, cutting her off.

"Do you have it?"

"Depends on the wood you need. But I'm sure we have it. Our warehouse is extensive," Roxanne replied with a huff.

"Rowan, yew, and ash—about one meter of each. Do you have these?" Quan asked, giving an expectant look at Roxanne. "Oh, and one other...steel core bamboo. Can you get all of these?"

"You want me to procure runed specimens of the three woods and just...what—hand them to you? These are some of the most powerful ingredients in our possession."

Quan gave her a tight smile. "Are you fond of Tristan?"

"I don't see how that pertains to this or is any of your business," Roxanne answered, looking flustered. "But yes, we are close, if you must know. Yes, yes, I'm quite fond of him."

"I'm fond of him too," Quan whispered and looked at Roxanne, searching her face. "We were close once long ago. Before I betrayed him, I loved him—as you do."

"Then why are you doing this?" Roxanne asked, her face turning crimson.

Quan looked at the cell that contained Monty. "Because I need his help. I need a battle mage with all his power to fight a creature you can't imagine in the worst of your nightmares"

"I don't see how the three woods can help. They are inert and require treatment. That would take days—" Roxanne started.

Quan held up a hand, silencing her. "If I don't form

a focus and get inside in time to facilitate the power shift—Tristan will be overwhelmed by his power, lose his mind, and go dark," Quan said matter-of-factly. "If he goes dark, I *will* have to kill him and most likely all of you, since you'll try to defend him. I would prefer to avoid that outcome if possible."

"You would destroy us all?" Cassandra asked, her voice trembling. "We would stop you."

Quan fixed Cassandra with a stare. My stomach clenched tight at her expression. In that moment, I knew. Not only would she do it, she could.

"Every *Ordaurum* is given an *umbra mortis*—a shadow death. It's a mage of equal or greater power from a separate sect who is chosen. They form an unbreakable pact. It binds them as long as they live. If either of the two goes dark, the other is tasked with elimination of the dark mage—with their life, if necessary. I am Tristan's as he's mine."

"What happens if they both go dark?" Roxanne asked quietly. "Then what?"

"They are both destroyed by the combined might of their sects. I would like to prevent Tristan from going dark. To do *that*, I need the three woods—now, please."

"I'll be right back," Roxanne answered, retrieving her key card. "I need to go to the other side of the facility. It may take a while."

Cassandra shot a wary glance at Quan. "I'll come with you. She creeps me the hell out."

They headed off to the elevator, moving fast. I saw the runes flare as they got on and left.

"I'm sure you get that a lot," I said, looking at the runes on the door. "I know Monty does. Can you really open it?"

"That mark on your hand...what does it do?" she asked while staring at it. "It radiates power, unlike the rest of you—which is strangely null."

I considered lying for a brief second, but thought against it.

"It allows me to stop time," I said while reaching for Grim Whisper. I turned and fired into the corner behind me. The entropy rounds punched into the darkness and a figure fell forward.

Quan walked over to the body. "A lurk." It was featureless and looked like a long slug with two large slits for eyes. "You have a Negomancer watching you. Only they employ these creatures."

"Beck," I said, prodding the lurk with a toe. The entropy rounds dissolved it into nothingness a few seconds later. "He's been after Monty since The Randy Rump."

"He will be close and on his way. Negomancers are never far from their spies. If I open the door without the focus, it will accelerate the shift." She examined the runes on the door again. "We must wait for the three woods."

"Have you ever fought a Negomancer?" I asked as she faced away from me, examining the runes. I saw the elevator arrive and I unsheathed Ebonsoul. It was way too soon for them to be back with the three woods.

"Once; they are difficult to dispatch. Negomancy is quite formidable and requires an immense amount of power to fight. It usually takes two to three mages to stop one Negomancer." She traced some of the runes near the floor with her finger. "I don't look forward to facing another one if I can avoid it."

"About that… I don't think we're going to be able to avoid it," I said as the elevator doors opened and Beck stepped out. "Do you think you can take on a Negomancer alone?"

She looked up as the runes flared around the elevator and then disappeared.

"Shite," she said. She stood up slowly. "This is Beck?"

I nodded and began firing.

THIRTY

My bullets made it about halfway to him before they fell to the floor in a pile of useless metal.

"I'm here for Tristan," Beck said as he approached. "Just hand him over and I'll be on my way." The runes flared red under his feet for a few seconds and then went black. "How did you spot my lurk, by the way?"

"We may need to give him what he wants," Quan whispered under her breath. "Keep him distracted."

"What do you mean by give him what he wants? And distract him with what? Sharp wit?"

"I'd say yes, but it seems you lack that, so try that blade of yours—it looks dangerous." She crouched down to examine the runes on the door to Monty's cell. "I need a few moments to get this door open. Go introduce yourself."

Beck looked like a university professor who had lost

his way to class. He wore a brown jacket, a beige shirt, and a complementing rust- colored tie. Khaki dress slacks finished off the ensemble. He looked normal except for his hands being covered in black energy and the black tears—the black tears were still unsettling.

"This one you *can* bite," I whispered to Peaches as we walked down the hallway to head Beck off. "Be careful. He's nasty."

<*Thank you! I'll only remove a leg or an arm. Nothing he needs.*>

Peaches bounded off and leaped, disappearing mid-jump. I unsheathed Ebonsoul and slid forward as Beck released a black orb at me. With nowhere to dodge, I raised Ebonsoul in front of me. It absorbed the orb and he raised an eyebrow in surprise.

"What kind of blade is that?" he asked squinting at Ebonsoul. "Where did you get this weapon?"

I took a step back into a defensive stance. "Do you need a tissue or something? I mean, really, the black tears don't work with the professor-look. Maybe a trench coat? Even a holocaust cloak would work."

He pulled out a blade in response. "Fine, you seem to be immune to my magic. I'll erase you the old way," he said and lunged.

"Cut first, cut fast, or die." Master Yat's words came to me as Beck's blade closed. I parried the lunge and sliced across, aiming for his thumb. He released his blade and caught it with the other hand, avoiding my slash. He bent forward and shot out a leg behind him, catching the reappearing Peaches in mid-air in the chest with the back-kick. A sickening crunch filled my ears and stole my breath. My heart lurched as Peaches

tumbled down the hallway and landed in front of the elevator. He didn't move.

"You'd better pray you didn't kill him, Beck," I said, my voice full of emotion as I advanced menacingly towards him.

"I'm a Negomancer. You can't sneak up on me. I sense and negate energy—all energy. You should have kept that creature away from me." He smirked. "But don't worry if he isn't dead. I'll put him out of his misery after I'm done with you."

He jumped back, formed another black orb, and slammed it into the floor. Any time Monty slammed magic into the floor it usually meant some earth-shattering event was about to happen. The devastation runes flared to life. A wave of light radiated outward from where he had slammed it down. I punched Beck in the face, knocking him on his back, and ran for Peaches. Beck began to laugh. The runes glowed brighter as I scooped up Peaches and dived into the elevator.

The devastation runes triggered and the world exploded.

THIRTY-ONE

I lay sprawled out in the elevator, partially covering Peaches. He was still breathing. The elevator was wrecked, along with my body, which was aching in new and unfamiliar places.

I slowly got to my feet and staggered out of the

elevator into a right cross that spun me clockwise and slammed my face into the wall. I slid down it, barely conscious, as the floor tilted beneath me. Darkness filled the edges of my vision and crept in as Beck came into focus.

"No one said you can't punch and kick in a knife fight," he said as he leaned in close to my face. "I'd take the extra time to kill you and your little dog, but I have orders. You aren't the target, Tristan is, and I have to deliver him to the Council. Dead or alive. I'm thinking he put up a struggle and had to be subdued—with lethal force."

"Fuck you, Beck," I managed, spitting out some blood. "Just give me a moment so I can kick your ass."

"Oh, you won't be healing anytime soon," he said and laughed as he stood. "I laced my energy into the devastation runes in the floor. Your immortality and your healing are on hold for a little while."

I glared at him as I tried to sit up properly but failed. He was right. My body wasn't reacting normally. None of the wounds closed and my head still rang from the punch.

"How did you; what happened, no...I mean, what did you do?" I stammered as my vision swam and the floor tilted under me again.

"If you know the enemy and you know yourself, you need not fear the results of a hundred battles," he whispered, crouching down next to me. "I do my homework, Strong. I saw your performance at the butcher shop. Granted, Tristan did all of the heavy lifting, but there was something off about you. I dug and found out all about the 'chosen of Kali.' It was sparse, but enough to neutralize you."

"Someone shared information they shouldn't have with you. Who was it?" I croaked and coughed up more blood. Every word felt like sandpaper with bits of broken glass massaging my throat as I tried to get the words out.

"Does it matter? It doesn't look like you're leaving this place—alive, at least."

He made a move to stand up. I shifted my weight and buried Ebonsoul in his thigh. I was aiming for his neck, but my current state of equilibrium made objects appear closer than they really were.

He fell back and screamed. I actually smiled. It was the best sound I'd heard all day. Black orbs formed in his hands as he whirled and homed in on me.

"Appear weak when you are strong and strong when you are weak," I said, standing shakily. "As far as magic-users go, Negomancers are amateurs."

He clenched his jaw, pulled out Ebonsoul and tossed it to one side with a grunt.

"I wasn't going to kill you, but you just became collateral damage." He launched the orbs at me. "Time to die."

The orbs froze mid-flight and evaporated. I looked over to Monty's cell and saw the door open and Quan casting a spell. I picked up Ebonsoul and scrambled over to the elevator, scooping up Peaches, and felt my body scream at me. I wasn't healing yet. When I stepped out of the elevator, Monty was walking toward us.

All around him, tendrils of violet energy bled off his body in a haze of flickering, purple flame, that was flecked throughout with shimmering specks of gold giving him the appearance of being on fire.

He gestured and a wall of energy materialized between us as Beck unleashed several orbs of black energy. They hit the wall with enough force to create tremors around us, but it held. I gave Monty a short nod as I passed him on my way to Quan.

"Where I come from, calling someone's heritage into question is a sign of poor breeding," Monty said and formed a flame orb in his hand.

"What the hell is that?" I asked Quan as I looked at the mini-sun in Monty's hand. "He's never created anything that bright."

After a few seconds, I had to look away.

"In the room—now!" She shoved me into the room and gestured with her hand, covering the doorway with semi-opaque energy. We fell in a pile as flames filled the entire sub-level.

"Did he just incinerate the entire sub-level? What is happening to him?" I asked as I grabbed the stunned Quan by the shoulder.

"A *corsolis*," she whispered in awe. "He unleashed a sun's heart, with just a thought."

"Why does that sound like a bad thing? It is a bad thing, right?"

"He shouldn't be able to cast that spell for at least another fifty years. The power shift is accelerating too fast—it will consume him," she said, her voice grim. I was about to step outside when she grabbed my arm.

"What?" I said, trying to pull away. "Beck might still be out there. I need to help Monty." She clamped down hard with a vise-grip and held me in place.

"Not yet, I need to undo Beck's attack or you *will* die if the *corsolis* is still active," she said and muttered some words under her breath.

Golden light shot down her arm and into mine. The light surrounded me as my body vibrated. Her hand trembled and I could tell it was a major effort for her to hold on. When she let go, I was launched into the nearest wall hard enough to make me gasp.

"A little warning next time would be great," I wheezed and then realized I felt better. The impact should have bruised and battered me but I was feeling better with each passing second. "I think it worked. Can you fix Peaches?"

She placed her hands on the side of Peaches' body and the same golden light cascaded over him. When she removed them, he slid a few feet and stopped.

"He should be fine," she said, shaking out her hands. "We need to see to Tristan."

"I'm curious. How come Peaches got a gentle nudge and I get the body-slam treatment?" I said as I peeked out of the doorway. I saw Monty lying face down in the hallway. Beck was near the elevator, unconscious. The same violet flames from before were filling the area around him.

"Because Peaches is a gentle, majestic creature, and you're not," she said as she stepped up next to me. She gestured and the wall of energy dissipated. A blast of power rushed into the room and nearly knocked me down. The airflow around us increased.

"Is this the corsolis effect?" I asked, raising my voice as the energy increased, making it hard to hear. She shook her head and pointed at Monty.

"This is part of the power shift. We need to get to Tristan before it gets worse." She headed down the hallway to where Monty lay.

"It gets worse?" I yelled, following her. This felt like walking in a hurricane, which I had always thought was a bad idea. She fell on one knee. When I reached down to help, I noticed that tendrils of energy had attached themselves to her. It was draining her magic.

She pulled me close. "We're running out of time. Your blade...You need to use your blade as a focus. It was the only way he was able to stop Beck even with the corsolis. Your blade weakened the Negomancer enough for Tristan to overwhelm him."

"My blade? What do you want me to do?"

She pointed to a spot above my abdomen. "There. You have to stab him there and hold it in place."

"You want me to stab Monty?" I said in disbelief.

"Only if you want him to live. Hurry," she said and fell back, unconscious. I placed her gently on the floor and made my way to Monty. He lay on his stomach so I turned him over. He was unconscious. His sweat-slicked hair covered part of his face. I moved it out of the way. His skin was clammy and pale, his mouth fixed in its usual scowl. I didn't think his facial muscles remembered how to form a smile.

I unsheathed Ebonsoul and looked down at my friend. The tendrils of violet energy swirled around me and slammed into the blade, making it hard to keep my grip. The force of the energy was building momentum. I was sitting in the eye of a cyclonic vortex and it *was* getting worse.

"Fuck, this sucks," I said under my breath, then

plunged Ebonsoul into his body.

THIRTY-TWO

I saw my hands burn first.

Ebonsoul was created to deal with supernatural threats. It rendered their abilities null and void evening the playing field. It also siphoned life force and channeled it into me. It wasn't meant to be a focus. The tendrils jumped from the blade to me and every muscle in my body contracted. The flow had reversed and now I was siphoning whatever Monty was going through.

Ebonsoul wasn't the focus; I was. My body couldn't take it as my arms burst into violet flame.

I managed to reach over with two fingers and touched my mark. White light shot out from the top of my left hand and everything came to a stop. Everything around me was slightly out of focus, but I couldn't move. My arms were still burning and the energy had crept up higher.

"That looks unpleasant," a voice said from behind me. "Are you testing your immortality?"

It was Karma. She stepped into my view and shook her head. She was wearing black leather with accents of black leather. Her boots creaked as she bent down to look into my face.

"Hello, Karma," I said with some effort. "Dominatrix looks good on you."

She gave me one of her predatory smiles and caressed my cheek. I flinched, expecting one of her skull-rocking taps, and she laughed.

"I was on my way to a mage dungeon not far from here and needed to look the part, when I sensed you. Seems they had some minor disaster and I need to go establish balance. It promises to be painful—for them."

"Speaking of balance, you think you can restore some here?" I said, craning my neck to look up at her. Sweat poured into my eyes from the effort. "This energy is too much for me."

"I noticed. Your weapon isn't designed to hold that much power, and frankly, neither are you—immortal or not." She frowned as she looked closer at Monty. "This isn't good."

"Really? What gave it away? The flames around my body or my blade sticking out of him?"

"That mouth of yours is going to get you killed one day, splinter," she said, and this time she did rock my skull with a brief slap. I flexed my jaw and shook my head until the spots cleared. I made a mental note not to let her punch me—ever.

"Whose bright idea was this?" she asked, looking at me. "Not even you in all your supposed brilliance would think to use your weapon in this manner."

"It was hers," I gestured at Quan with my head. "Made sense at the time."

"Stabbing a mage going through a power shift into ascendance with a siphoning weapon created to combat the supernatural made *sense* to you?" she said and grabbed my face. "This is a special kind of stupid, Simon."

"When you put it that way it does sound bad." I stared back at her. "But he's in trouble and I had to do something. I'm not just going to let him go dark and die alone."

She stood up and shook her head slowly. "No. It looks like you're going to join him."

"Can you stop it?" I asked. "Or at least slow it down until Roxanne gets here with the three woods?"

"No. I can't alter this. It has to run its course. If I remove the blade—he goes dark and who knows what happens to you." She stepped close and placed a hand on my shoulder. "All I can do is help you hold on, but you must not remove the blade. Do you understand?"

"I'll take any help I can get," I whispered, struggling to form the words through the searing pain. Tears streamed uncontrollably down my face as the flames inched up my arms.

"Not all help is beneficial—remember that." She vanished as time snapped back, along with the force of the energy hurricane, threatening to rip me away from Monty. I noticed a golden lattice around my hands and Ebonsoul. It was the only thing keeping me in place. Well, that and the fact that Ebonsoul was buried in Monty's abdomen.

Through the haze of pain, I noticed movement beside me. It was Quan. I saw her gesture around something but I couldn't make out what she was doing. There was something about being on fire that tends to distract you from anything happening around you. My body was losing the battle in the healing arena and I didn't think I could hold on much longer, when Quan stepped into my view.

"This is going to hurt—a lot," she said and I could tell she held something in her hand. "Get ready." She crouched down low, rotated her body, and slammed a palm into my chest. I went airborne and slammed into the wall at the other end of the hallway with bone-breaking force. I knew this because I felt a few ribs crack as I fell to the floor.

I saw her take a short staff —similar to the one Master Yat used—and thrust it into the floor. The cyclonic energy around Monty streamed into the staff. After what felt like a lifetime, but was probably only a minute, at most, it stopped. As it dissipated, she fell to her knees with a relieved sigh.

I shifted my weight to stand and my side screamed at me, letting me know it was a bad idea. I let my body begin the healing process, rested my head against the wall, and closing my eyes, slipped away into unconsciousness.

Sometime later, a large tongue slapped me wetly across my face. I opened an eye to see Peaches staring at me balefully as I felt his drool begin to stiffen on my cheek.

<I don't think this is naptime. Do you need me to bite you so you can get up?>

"No, thanks. I must have passed out," I muttered as I stood slowly. "Weren't you napping a little while ago?"

<That's different. That was battle fatigue. He kicked me, and it hurt inside. Can I take a bite out of him now? He's taking a nap too.>

"Stay away from him for now," I said as I shuffled over to where Monty sat with Quan. "He's dangerous and I don't want you getting hurt again."

He gave me a short grumble as he padded next to

me.

<Doesn't look like he would taste good anyway.>

"Are you speaking to your dog?" Cassandra said from behind me with a smirk. "Does he talk back?"

"Actually, he does. When did you get here? *How* did you get here? The elevator is trashed." I looked around. I located Roxanne near a stairwell directing staff onto the floor around the wreckage. "I don't remember there being stairs leading down here."

"That's because it was a black site. We put in the stairs in case the elevator malfunctioned," Roxanne said as she came close and examined and prodded me. In addition to being a sorceress, she was also a doctor. "You have multiple contusions, a few cracked ribs, from the feel of things, and second-degree—now first-degree—burns on both your arms. You should be fine in a few minutes."

Cassandra stood transfixed. She stared at my arms as they healed. "What the hell are you?" She pointed at my arms as the skin repaired itself and tissue reknit over the wounds.

"You ever hear of Wolverine?" I said as I borrowed a jacket from one of the Haven staff.

"Who?" she said, taking a step back. I was used to this reaction from anyone who saw what my body did when I was injured. The list of EMTs I've creeped out was a mile long.

"The patron saint of badassery? He's a mutant with crazy healing ability. I have that same condition. My body heals abnormally fast. That's all." I shrugged.

"Bullshit, Wolverine is a character from a comic book. How stupid do you think I am? Healing condition, my ass." She pointed at my chest. "Tell me the truth."

"Fine, the truth," I said, shaking my head. "I pissed off a goddess who is probably the *most* powerful magic-user on the planet and she cursed me alive in a fit of rage. That is why my body heals the way it does."

Cassandra just stared at me. "You just don't know when to be serious? Look around you. This shit just got real. Your friend almost died—we all almost died, and you're making jokes? I'll be upstairs. Ramirez will want to be in the loop." She stormed off and up the stairs.

"I—but…ugh," was all I could manage as she disappeared.

"Such eloquence," Monty said with a groan as he stood and leaned on a staff. His midsection was bandaged but, other than a few scrapes, he looked fine. "Let her have some space, Simon. She needs to process all of this and it's not easy."

"She needs to process? I'm still trying to figure out what happened." I pointed at his bandage. "Sorry about the stabbing—Quan said it was the right thing to do."

"It wasn't the most painless solution" —he gave her a sidelong glance—"but it did help, at least until I got this." He held up the staff.

"Wait, no way. Are you like Monty the White now? Kickass mage extraordinaire—Gandalf level?"

"Is he always this way?" Quan asked as she helped Monty to the stairs. "I could seal him down here for a few millennia?"

Monty shook his head. "He'd find a way to escape.

There is no color attribution to mage ascendancy, Simon," he said with a sigh. "The outcome is simple. You gain more power or it consumes you. In which case you go mad and dark."

"And get eliminated," Quan added with a whisper. "Don't forget that part."

"What happened, Monty? One moment you were fine and the next, whoosh—violet flames everywhere," I said, looking at the staff. "Is this the three woods?"

The dark wood gave off a subdued violet light. Three pieces of wood were wrapped around a fourth to form a whole.

"I need this for a little while" —he held up the short staff—"at least until the power regulates within my body. My apologies for the barbeque." He gestured to my arms. "I thought I was dealing with an erasure, not a shift."

"What does it do? I mean, besides look badass and make you debonair?"

"It's a repository," he said. "Some magic is too powerful, especially during ascendancy. Objects can be imbued with power and they can take the strain when we can't." He hefted the staff in one hand. "This also acts as a force multiplier, amplifying the power of any spell I cast."

"That's like the Chicago wizard. He uses a staff, except his is bigger. I'm sure that's not an indication of power. Now that you have one, does this make you a *wizard*?" I asked, gesturing to the staff. "Is there a term for a mage with a staff? Magerd? Wizage?"

He glanced in my direction and my Armani suit jacket disintegrated. "I've been looking for a reason to try this particular spell of unbinding. It works on a molecular level, but it's highly unstable. I wonder how it would affect someone who is cursed alive?" He gave me a look as he rubbed his chin. "Would the curse keep you whole or would you fly apart like your jacket?"

"That sounds excruciating," I said, putting my hands up in mock surrender. "Let's not. That was an Armani by the way. Can I have it back?"

He gestured and my jacket reassembled around me. "Call me a wizard again and we can test the limits of your curse," he said as we reached the main level and my phone went off.

"Strong, we have a problem—a large one," Ramirez said, his voice strained. "I have packs of Werewolves roaming the city. I don't even want to imagine what this turns into in a few days."

"Do you have enough restraints?" I checked my inside pocket to make sure I had mine. "You're going to need to make them stronger."

"I have Jhon working on them now and he's making something else—a runic inhibitor, or something like that, supposed to be better than the restraints," he said and grew quiet. "Strong, this is looking bad. Tell me you and the mage have a plan, or an army. Because the brass is thinking of razing them all and starting fresh."

"Are you insane?" I whispered and turned my back. "That's genocide. You can't just eliminate all of them."

"We don't have the manpower to deal with a full-on Werewolf revolt," he replied. "In case you haven't noticed, humans don't possess supernatural abilities. The NYTF doesn't have enough silver to deal with this."

"They're reacting in fear. You're the director, goddammit, *direct* them, Angel," I hissed. "You can't let them do this. Every time we face a danger, we're just going to wipe out everyone? What happened to secure, contain, and protect?"

"That…was a beautiful speech, Strong. So much passion. I'll make sure to repeat it to them when they order the destruction of *all* Werewolves, to protect the *humans* in the city. I'm sure they'll see things your way."

"Fuck," I said under my breath. "Give me until the full moon. If we haven't put a stop to this by then it won't matter."

"I agree. By then those of us left will be fighting for our lives. One other thing—stop scaring the shit out of my lieutenant. She called me, spouting some nonsense about gods and how you can self-heal in seconds while you grow back skin."

"It was a harmless prank." I looked over to where Cassandra stood and I waved. She gave me the stink-eye and turned away. She was on the phone, having an animated conversation of her own. I had a good guess as to whom she was speaking with.

"You have three days, Strong, or they release their final solution," he said slowly. "And it won't matter if I'm the director or not if we're all dead."

He ended the call and I looked up and caught Monty's eye. He walked over with Quan and Roxanne beside him.

"How bad?" Monty asked as he leaned on his staff.

"Does the NYTF possess any artifact that could eliminate *all* of the Werewolves? Something they would consider a 'final solution' if they felt it was the only way to deal with a threat? You know, something the mages may have overlooked after the war?" I gave him a look.

He rubbed his chin. "Not to my knowledge. We determined the negation rune belonged to a private collector, which is why the MCRU missed it. But something that can specifically target lycanthropes? I don't think so."

"Are you sure? There isn't a spell, a rune, or something that kills only Werewolves?"

"Nothing I've heard of," he said, still rubbing his chin. "If there was, it would require a complex spell with a simple delivery system. A mage would need to create a 'smart spell' to target a specific species."

"There is," Roxanne said quietly.

THIRTY-THREE

"It's a silver-nitrate-based airborne contagion," Roxanne said. "The government was working on it a few years back—it's called AGNO-3. They wanted a way to deal with the Werewolf population if they ever became a threat."

"I thought silver nitrate was harmful to humans too?" I said. "If they release that into the air, they'll kill humans."

"Those will be called 'acceptable losses' if it eliminates *all* of the Werewolves," Monty said and then looked at Roxanne.

"No, it was created with magic-users," Roxanne

answered and pulled out her phone. "AGNO-3 will target only lycanthropes. That's how it's designed."

"Do you have any of this AGNO-3?" Monty asked, his voice grim. His knuckles turned white as he gripped his staff.

"Every supernatural detention facility carries a small amount of it on site in case of a Werewolf going rogue or attacking the staff," she said before calling a staff member over. "It's always a last resort since the effects are lethal. We keep it secure on the medical wing."

"I need to see it," Monty said.

Roxanne nodded, then spoke to the staff member who approached. "Lydia will direct you to where it's kept. I need to coordinate with teams downstairs. Sub-level four will be shut down for the duration."

"What about Beck?" I said. She gave me a look of confusion. "Professor dark and nasty? Looks like he's having the worst mascara day in history? Fires black orbs of energy?"

"The Negomancer," she said with sudden realization. "He will be returned to the Dark Council. We don't want him here."

"He tried to erase Monty," I said in disbelief as Roxanne rummaged through her pockets. "He was going—"

"He was doing his job," she said placing her hands on her hips. "What do you suggest I do? Place him in a cell and forget he exists? This is not a black site anymore. We don't 'disappear' people, Simon."

"I just thought that he should be held for a while," I said. "Just until we get this all sorted out."

"You thought wrong. We have no jurisdiction to

hold him. If I do that, I have to deal with the Council —no, thank you. I need to get downstairs and oversee this disaster. Before I go"—she turned to Quan and gave her a hug—"thank you for saving him."

Judging from the surprise on Quan's face, hugs were not a usual thing. She was probably more a 'punch to your throat' kind of woman.

"You're welcome," Quan answered, awkwardly returning the hug. "You did help, you know. Without the three woods, it would have been for nothing."

Roxanne stepped close to Monty and gently touched his face. "It's good to have you back," she whispered. "Try to stay in one piece, yes?"

He put his hand on hers and nodded as she headed off downstairs to sub-level four.

"Suave, Monty," I said with a grin. "You should write a self-help book on relationships. Call it *'The Eloquence of Silence'* or something like that."

He gave me the one-finger-salute as he followed Lydia and Quan to the elevators. I was about to join them, when my phone went off again. Monty looked at me sharply. It was the one ringtone I dreaded hearing —the "Imperial March" and only the Hack used it. I didn't even set it up for him. He just managed to have it play that way every time he called. I waved Monty and Quan ahead and connected the call.

"Hack, this is a bad time." I put it on speakerphone and braced for the convoluted response I called Hackspeak. "What's up?"

"Completely bad, Simon!" he yelled. "Completely!"

"Hack, take a breath and pretend I don't know what you're talking about," I said slowly. "What is going on?"

"I was recalibrating my runic filter and there's a spike...a spike! I have ghost particles dancing with Majorana. My runic filter detects spikes in magic-use and there's...there's a tear!" he said all in one breath. "In the middle of the city! This is bad...oh, this is bad."

"Hack, I don't know who the Major is or what ghosts in the machine you're referring to. Can you start over again, in English this time?"

"Middle of the city. Tear in space-time. Tiny now, but it's starting to grow. Think of a magical black hole, only on steroids. Will swallow everything. Maybe it's a door?"

"How long, Hack? How long before it starts to grow?" I knew what he was talking about and it chilled my blood. The words 'magical black hole' reminded me of how Monty dealt with Slif.

"Maybe a few days, maybe a year. I don't know! Leave now while you can. Hack out!" He hung up.

Cassandra stood a few feet away and gave me an icy stare. "What was that? What tear and where is this tear?" she demanded, looking around as if the floor was about to open up into a chasm beneath us.

"How's George doing?" I asked, deflecting her question and putting my phone away. "Is he still with the NYTF?"

"How did you—how did you know who I was talking to?" she said with a puzzled look. "He's retired now That sounded bad. Do you know what he meant?"

"Unfortunately, yes," I replied as I looked up and saw Monty and Quan running our way. Behind them, my eyes saw the image, but my brain refused to process what my eyes saw and declared it a hallucination. A pack of angry Werewolves was chasing Monty.

THIRTY-FOUR

Peaches growled next to me and squared off in attack mode as Monty and Quan approached. I grabbed Cassandra by the arm and made for the entrance to the building.

"What are you doing?" Cassandra tried to shrug off my hand. "Let go of me! What the hell?"

<More behind us. These are bad dogs.>

"Stay close, boy," I said under my breath. "Those are extremely bad dogs."

The howls behind me indicated the entrance was blocked. Monty and Quan caught up. The Werewolves at the entrance remained outside—trapping us inside.

"Good news," Monty said as he caught his breath. "We won't have to find Davros."

"And the bad news?" I asked, taking a quick count of the Werewolves around us and losing track after twenty. "That is a buttload of Werewolves."

"You do realize that a 'buttload' is a unit designed to measure liquid?" Monty said and pushed some hair from his face.

"Thank you, WikiMonty." I drew Grim Whisper and held out my hand. Monty passed me the last two magazines of entropy rounds. "The bad news?"

"We won't have to find Davros, because he found us," he said as the Werewolves parted.

"What do you mean he found us?" I said, looking at the parting pack of Werewolves. A figure stepped through the gap. "That's one hell of an entrance."

"He always was a bit full of himself," Monty said under his breath. "Remember he's not too stable."

Davros was an imposing presence. Standing almost as tall as Monty, he wore a dark suit with an off-white shirt that would have made Piero proud. His dirty blond hair was cut short on the sides and long on top. His eyes were the bluest I had ever seen.

When I looked into them, I realized two things: One —he was about as stable as a two-legged stool on thin ice. Two—we were fucked. I pushed open my coat and made sure I had access to the bullets and blade. Somehow, I knew they weren't going to be enough. The wind started to pick up around us, which felt odd since we were inside the lobby of the building.

"I'm not sensing the Phoenix Tail," Quan whispered. "He doesn't have it with him. This isn't good."

"Monty," I said under my breath as Davros approached, "he's gone way past unstable into batshit-crazy territory. We need to get some fighting room before he unleashes this pack on us."

"I'm working on it. Just try to stay indoors," Monty whispered back and adjusted his staff in his hands. He focused on Davros, who stood about twenty feet away. "How did you find us?"

"Find you?" Davros said with a crooked smile. "Are you joking, Tristan? No, you never did have a sense of humor. You opened a *void vortex* in the middle of Manhattan. We can find you anywhere you go after that. You've marked yourself and probably destroyed the city."

Monty shifted his staff around on the floor. "Who's *we*?" he asked matter-of-factly.

"Yeah, about that," I whispered as I turned and unholstered Grim Whisper. "Hack said there's a tear in space-time and it's growing."

"That would be bad," Monty answered, still moving his staff on the floor. "Catastrophic."

"Worse than getting shredded by these Werewolves?"

Monty gave me a short nod. "Infinitely worse. We have to go close it, before Slif returns."

"Okay, just wanted to know the priority here," I said and looked at him. "This isn't looking too good, Monty."

"We've seen worse, haven't we?" he said, his voice grim, and I nodded.

"Do you know what precious metal most hospitals have an abundance of?" Davros asked, spreading his arms wide. "It's quite amazing, really, how much I found just lying about."

"Oh, shit," I said when I realized what he meant. Davros laughed. It was actually closer to a cackle and it set my teeth on edge. "He's controlling those Werewolves pretty well, isn't he?"

Monty grimaced. "Seems he found platinum." He ran his hand through his hair and squinted at Davros. "The Permutation is almost complete."

"Can you take him?" I asked, as I made sure I had easy access to Ebonsoul.

"We'll find out, won't we?" Monty raised his staff.

"Confidence—that's what I'm talking about, Monty,"

I said as I turned and fired.

THIRTY-FIVE

Davros laughed and slammed his hands together. The entropy rounds dispersed. They flew in every direction except the one I wanted—toward Davros. I felt the shockwave before I saw it. The air grew thin and I felt the whump in my stomach. I pressed the main bead on the mala as Monty slid his staff across the floor, trailing runes in its wake.

Quan grabbed Cassandra and jumped behind me as the wave of energy crashed into us and ejected us through the window and into the street. We stood up, unharmed, but the lobby was obliterated. Several Werewolves lay dead around us. The rest started closing in on where we stood.

Lightning hit a car next to us and punched a hole through the engine and into the ground, crushing it. The wind howled, whipping the rain as it began to cascade around us.

"I thought you said he was erased?" I winced at another lightning strike that hit twenty feet away. I was acutely aware that the mala shield had dropped. "This doesn't look erased. This looks like he has full command of his abilities."

"Drake's blood," Monty said. "It can awaken dormant powers. Rumors say it can undo an erasure." Monty raised his staff. A bolt of lightning hit it and he redirected the energy into the ground. Davros walked outside, trailed by the pack of Werewolves. "I'm inclined to believe the rumors at this point."

"You left me, Tristan. Abandoned me," Davros said and formed an angry orb of electricity in his hand. "You let them erase me—strip me of my power, and throw me in a box. You left me there to die."

"You needed to be stopped," Monty whispered, looking around as his jaw clenched. "You were out of control. You killed—you killed so many senselessly. We —I—had to stop you." He flexed his hand. "Look around you. How many more have to die?"

"What I *needed* was my sect brother to stand by my side!" Davros screamed, pointing at Monty. "I needed you to understand. These Werewolves are like the others—aberrations that need to be purged. They aren't pure—they're wrong—mistakes that need to be corrected. Magic belongs to us, not to these—these *things*."

I stepped back from Davros, who reminded me of a human Tesla coil at this point. "Monty, I think the train has left the station but the conductor is nowhere to be found. That orb looks nasty."

"You think I'm crazy?" Davros said, looking at me, his eyes wild. "I'm not crazy. A crazy person knows when they're crazy, right?"

"No you're not crazy," I said calmly with one hand up. I unsheathed Ebonsoul with the other, since bullets weren't going to help here. "Maybe we can help you."

"I'm the only one who sees everything clearly. If we don't get rid of them—they took everything from me," Davros said, rushing the words. "Don't you understand? I have to do this—I have to. It's the only way. The only way!"

I glanced at Monty and nodded. "Wait, maybe there's another way. We can sit down and figure this out. Right, Monty?"

Monty nodded back, his lips tight. "Davros, you need help. Let us help you. We can get through this."

"Help me? Help me. Help me!" Davros said gasping between each plea. He began crying and then was, quite suddenly, laughing hysterically. "Where were you when I needed help? No, no, you won't help."

"I want to help you, Davros. Let me help you." Monty took a step forward. "We can end this."

"You don't want to help me—you want to erase—erase me again. The dragons. The dragons helped me, gave me power. Power you took away," Davros said, and then he did something that scared me more than any of his words. He grew quiet and stared at us. "No more help—time for you to die." Glancing at the werewolves, he gestured towards us. "Kill them!"

The Werewolves howled as one and lunged at us.

"There's no reasoning with him," Monty said as the Werewolves closed on us. "I'm going to have to subdue him."

"What gave it away? The rant of madness, or that he just sicced a pack of mindless, homicidal Werewolves on us?"

"How droll," Monty said as he flexed his hand. "Dispatch them as quickly as possible. The Permutation isn't complete, but he may have many more under his control."

"Fine, how do you want to do this?" Quan said and undid the sash around her waist with a metallic ring.

She shook it out and the sections fell into place, forming a flexible sword.

"You and Simon take the Werewolves. I'll deal with Davros. I suggest the lieutenant take up the rear guard."

"Don't have to tell me twice." Cassandra backed up and drew her weapon. It was a Taurus Tracker Model 627 in .357 Magnum. It made Grim Whisper look like a Grim Whimper.

"You plan on going bear-hunting after this?" I said, shocked at the size of her hand-cannon. "That's not NYTF standard issue."

"No. Today I'm hunting wolves," she said with a grin. "My dad gave this to me the day I joined the NYTF. Said I might need it."

"Can you fire that thing without breaking your wrist?"

"Distinguished Marksman, Pistol, and Inter-Division Pistol," she said with a nod. "Been firing weapons almost before I could walk. Where do you want me?"

"Back there with Peaches," I said quickly. "Any of them get past or around us, you put them down. Whatever you do—don't get scratched or bitten. Understand?"

She nodded. "The Beast and I are clean-up. Don't get clawed or chewed on, roger that."

"Peaches, keep her safe. Don't let any of the bad dogs get to her," I said, hoping he understood. He rumbled at me and stood by her side in 'pounce and shred' mode.

< *As long as she remains by my side, I will keep the scared female safe from the bad dogs.* >

I heard Davros laugh again. "Tristan! Come erase me if you dare!" he yelled and released the orb.

The orb sped at us, growing in size. Monty ran toward it as another bolt of lightning came his way. The orb and the bolt reached him at the same time. An ear-splitting crack filled the street a second later, and Monty was gone.

THIRTY-SIX

I didn't have time to register what happened to Monty before a claw tried to eviscerate me. I leaped back and ducked under another swipe. These Werewolves were dangerous but slower than the ones I remembered facing. The mind-control of the Permutation slowed them down but made them relentless.

I twisted around another lunge and slid into Quan's hand as she shoved me back and removed a Werewolf arm and head in one smooth stroke. I stepped to the side and slashed down with Ebonsoul, stopping another attack from the side. I glanced quickly at Cassandra, who stood ready to blow away anything that got too close.

That momentary distraction almost cost me my head. A Werewolf slashed at my neck, and I saw it too late. I brought up Ebonsoul, but I knew those razor-sharp claws were going to dig into my flesh. An orb of energy blasted the Werewolf, forcing the slash high and raking my cheek instead.

"Keep your wits about you or lose your head," Quan

said as she dispatched another Werewolf. "There are too many of them. Davros can't be doing this. The dragon must be close. If Tristan doesn't act soon we will be overrun."

I peered into the building but didn't see Monty. It didn't help that Werewolves were lunging at us from every direction.

The burning sensation followed by the intense itching let me know my face was healing. I raced to Cassandra and Peaches as several Werewolves closed in. I removed the leg of one and stabbed through the neck of another. Peaches pounced on another. He shredded through its throat in one bite. Ebonsoul siphoned the power and channeled it to me. I removed three more, but they kept coming.

Cassandra fired her hand-cannon a few times, putting down several more. Quan was right, at this rate we were going to be overcome by Werewolves. I looked down the street and saw a figure surrounded by energy.

It was Slif.

"Quan!" I pointed up the street. She followed my arm and nodded. Her sword sang in the night as she cut a swath through the Werewolves as the pack trailed after her. I stood in front of Cassandra and Peaches as Slif released a blazing orange orb in our direction. I held up Ebonsoul, expecting to absorb it. It was a mistake. The orb punched through my chest and crashed into Cassandra behind me. We both flew back several feet with the force of the blast and bounced on the street. My body dealt with the wound immediately as my chest seized and pain shot through me.

Cassandra wasn't so lucky. She coughed a few times

—a wet, broken sound. Peaches came over, licked her face, and sat next to us in 'defend and shred' mode. I crouched down and removed the charred pieces of her jacket. The damage of her wound was gut wrenching and I clenched my jaw. Most of the left side of her chest was gone. Her chest cavity was crushed and she was losing too much blood. She must have seen the expression on my face.

"That bad, huh?" she wheezed and held my hand. "Take this and give it to my dad."

It was the .357 Magnum.

"I'll get Ramirez down here—we can rush a unit. Stay with me, Lieutenant." I placed the gun next to me. "You did great. Your dad would be proud of you. Hang with me. You're going to make it."

"Anyone ever tell you you're a shit liar?" she said with a grin that quickly became a grimace as the pain gripped her. "You tell my dad what I did. I held my ground and I kicked ass. Make sure—make sure you tell him."

"I will," I whispered, looking into her now vacant, lifeless eyes. "I'll make sure he knows. I'll make sure he's proud of you."

I closed her eyelids, picked up her gun and stood up. I heard the sirens in the distance, but they weren't going to get here in time. At least not for Cassandra, and not for the dozens of broken, bleeding bodies that lay in the street. All of the remaining Werewolves were chasing after Quan, who closed on Slif.

Even though Slif was the immediate threat, Davros was the closest one. I rushed into the lobby of the building as a fireball screamed past me and crashed into the street.

Monty held his staff in one hand and formed an orb of white flame with the other. He threw it and stood behind a column as I jumped over debris to join him. The resulting explosion echoed through the lobby.

"Where are the Werewolves?" he asked as he batted another fire orb away. "Where's Quan and the lieutenant?"

"Quan went to have a conversation with Slif, hopefully a violent one. The lieutenant...she didn't make it," I said, looking at her gun. "Slif hit me with something that Ebonsoul didn't absorb. Punched through me, and she was standing—"

"Behind you. Goddammit, Slif," he said, angry. "This is why dragons were hunted in the past. The power-plays and hidden agendas. Toying with humans until they grew bored, leaving death and destruction in their wake."

"Well, she's back. Seems she didn't like the cold that much. I also think *she's* controlling the Permutation, not Davros," I said as another fireball sailed by me. "Quan said she didn't feel the Phoenix Tail with him. What are you going to do about Davros? Are you going to kill him?"

"No. Something worse," he said, handing me his staff. "I'm going to erase his power, again."

"Monty," I said, holding out the staff as it vibrated with energy, "don't you kind of need this?"

"Not anymore," he said, his voice tight as violet tendrils surrounded him. "It's served its purpose. My power shift is done. It's time I serve *my* purpose."

I looked down at the staff and saw it turn gray and

then it crumbled in my hands. The pieces fell to the ground and became dust seconds later, blowing away into the street. Monty stepped away from the column and into the path of another fire orb. The orb raced at him and stopped suddenly.

The light of the flames shone against his face, and I saw his eyes. Golden circles ringed his irises, which had gone black. He looked down at the fire orb, extended a hand, and absorbed it.

"Monty? Monty?" I really hoped he hadn't gone *terminator*. This would be a bad time for him to lose his mind. "Are you there?"

"Of course I'm here. Where else would I be?" he snapped at me as black energy covered his hands. "Now, stay back. This is the first time I've tried this."

"That looks like the energy Beck uses," I whispered, taking a few steps back and taking cover behind another column. "You're going to negate Davros?"

"It's either that or kill him. I prefer to avoid taking his life." He walked forward. I followed a few paces behind him.

"Where's your staff, *wizard*?" Davros mocked as he came close. "You plan on killing me, Tristan?"

"I plan on helping you," Monty said as golden energy laced itself through the black orbs in his hands. "You need help. Let me help you. I can help you if you let me."

Davros shook his head as he formed black energy orbs of his own. "This is my life—my life! I'll live it how I choose and it will end the way *I* want it to end."

"Monty—that sounds bad," I said, drawing Grim Whisper. "He doesn't sound like he wants help. Sounds like he wants to end it all, and by 'all' I think he's including us."

Davros rushed at us and released an orb. My hand was on the mala bead before he took the first step. The orb smashed into my shield and dissolved it. Davros had reached Monty and I didn't have a shot. Monty's orbs were gone as Davros gestured with a hand and enclosed them both in a cloud of black energy.

I noticed the debris start tumbling toward them as the wind reversed direction. I remembered this feeling. It felt like being on the edge of the void vortex. I knew Monty wouldn't open another one, but it was possible Davros would.

"Let's go, boy!" I yelled to Peaches as we raced away from the lobby. He kept pace with me as we jumped over the destruction Davros had caused earlier with his shockwave. We made it to the street as the lobby exploded in black energy.

THIRTY-SEVEN

I stood shakily and saw Monty carrying Davros as he walked out of the building. I limped over to where he stood.

"Is he…?"

"He tried to unleash a void vortex," Monty said and gently laid him down on the ground. "I couldn't stop it before it drained him. He's gone. His mind was gone when he was erased after the war. The drake blood only made it worse. It gave him power but twisted him further."

"Why would they do this?" I looked up the street. The Werewolves were nowhere to be seen. Davros must've been crucial to the Permutation. With him gone, the Permutation stopped. "The Werewolves are gone."

"But the dragon isn't," Monty said and narrowed his eyes as he looked up the street. "You wanted to know why they would do this? Let's go ask a dragon."

We ran up the street as a flaming figure raced toward us. At first, I thought it was Slif. The fact that it lacked wings or a tail changed my mind. Monty released an orb of water, slowing it down and dousing the flames as he caught the body. It was Quan.

"There's an angry dragon up the street, Tris," she said through a wheeze. Burns covered her face and arms. "I tried to stop her. Don't think I even slowed her down. She has the Tail and the platinum. She only needs a vessel for the blood."

"Which means she can start the Permutation again?" I asked in disbelief. Quan nodded.

"Tristan, you have to stop her. Together, you can— you can stop her," she said before losing consciousness.

Her robe was torn and scorched. Large tears in the fabric revealed angry, red burn marks. Severe burns covered most of her body, but the thin, reedy sound escaping her blistered lips let me know she was still alive, still breathing.

"Can you heal these?" I asked Monty, looking at the burns all over her body. I felt the anger race through me but I kept it in check. I would let it loose, just not now.

"She went up against Slif alone," he whispered and held her head as he narrowed his eyes and examined her. "The burns are too widespread. I don't know. It may be too late. She's in a critical condition and its deteriorating rapidly."

"But you'll try," I said with certainty. "Let me help. I brought Quan into this. If she dies, it's my fault. I couldn't help Cassandra."

I pulled out my flask of Valhalla Java. Monty gave me the 'Are you an idiot?' stare. It glowed in the night, the blue skulls grinning at me with power as I uncapped it.

"You think this is the moment for a stiff one? Really?"

"This isn't alcohol. It's like WD-40 for your brain. I'll explain later." I poured about a vial's worth into Quan's mouth. "Try and help her now."

Monty just stared at me for a few seconds. "What did you give her?" he whispered as he placed his hands on her body. Golden light cascaded onto her and enveloped her in a cocoon of light. Monty raised an eyebrow in surprise. "Whatever is in that—WD40, it's working. What *did* you give her? Where did you get it?"

"Dragon?" I said. I looked up the street and put the flask away. "We have to deal with this before the city is swallowed by a black hole, remember?"

He placed Quan in safe location and made another gesture. An orange rune-covered sphere instantly surrounded her.

"She should be safe until she heals. Let's go have a conversation with a dragon," he said, pulling on his sleeves.

"Only if 'conversation' means giving Slif lots of pain and ending her," I said, standing and drawing Grim Whisper.

"That is what I had in mind, yes."

<Can I bite the big snake-woman now? She hurt the scared woman.>

"Boy, you go to town and shred that dragon," I said as I rubbed Peaches' head.

<Shred the dragon. Yes, I will shred her.>

He shook his body and barked. The sound shattered the nearby windows and rocked the cars around us. He expanded and grew more muscular as runes flared along his body. His hardened claws took chunks out of the asphalt with each step as he took off toward Slif.

"Perfect. Let's go converse," I said and took off at a dead run toward a fire-breathing dragon.

THIRTY-EIGHT

Slif, still in human form, turned at the sound of our approach. She smiled as we drew closer. I started firing as soon as I felt I was close enough not to miss. The entropy rounds never reached her, melting before they hit. She opened her mouth and a stream of flame raced at me. I leaped to the side as she laughed. I felt the heat even as I rolled away. Peaches stayed back when he saw me roll to the side.

Monty unleashed several black orbs, which hit her square in the chest but did nothing. She looked down at where the orbs hit and she brushed off her clothes.

"You think you can stand against me?"

I holstered Grim Whisper. "We can and will. You're nothing but an overgrown lizard with an inflated ego."

"I am a dragon, revered in every culture since the beginning of time," she said with a sneer. "We roamed the earth when you stupid primates barely had language."

"I think I see the problem here," I said, taking a cue from Monty. If magic-users were touchy, dragons had to be ten times worse. "We outgrew you. No one worships dragons anymore. I mean, sure, we like the image, but worship? Waste of time. What can a dragon do for me besides barbeque some meat or keep me warm in the winter?"

"We were manipulating matter while you were playing with dirt. You owe us everything." She took a deep breath.

"All you are is an overrated space heater," I shot back and pointed. "We don't need you, and this just pisses you off, doesn't it, oh mighty dragon? You can go suck—"

Another blast of flame erupted from her mouth and forced me to jump to the side.

"Today you will die for your arrogance," she rasped and transformed. The next moment I was standing in front of Smaug-lite and she looked pissed. "What's the matter, Simon? You look scared."

"I am scared," I admitted pulling out Ebonsoul. "But that isn't going to stop me from ending you today."

The heat shield around her dropped. Probably something to do with all the surface area she had in this form. Once Peaches realized the heat was gone, he leaped and latched on to a leg she lifted to fend him off. He clamped down and started shaking his head. He was taking the shredding command seriously. She tried to shake him off but failed.

"What did you do with William?" Monty asked as he traced runes around him in rapid motion. "Tell me where he is."

"He came to warn you and I buried him on his island north of here. He was a fool who thought he could stand against me. So I killed him." Slif grimaced as Peaches clamped down harder. "The same way I'm going to kill you."

"Wrong answer," Monty whispered through clenched teeth. "I will see you dead this night, dragon."

Monty placed his hands together and muttered under his breath. Whatever he said must have been dangerous because it got her attention in a hurry. She whipped her tail around and slammed Monty into a wall.

"We're wiping the slate clean," she said as she drove her leg into a wall and scraped Peaches off. "The Werewolves were just the start. But we will eliminate them all."

She crawled over to where I stood and loomed over me. Her teeth were easily the size of my arms. Her claws were the size of small cars and her body coiled around me. She peered down at me with her yellow eyes ringed with red to match her scales. Dragons—up close—were truly, unmistakably, petrifying.

"Who's *we*?" I said as I took out my flask of Valhalla Java. If I was going out, I was going to do it on my terms. I downed the entire flask and felt the liquid burn through my system. It was coffee heaven and I think my brain melted just a bit.

She took a breath, her cheeks filling with air and reminding me of old Louis Armstrong photos. It's amazing the things you'll remember when you're about to be reduced to ashes. I could feel the heat, and the air around me shimmering as she prepared to unleash a blast of instant sun.

I pressed my mark and everything became unfocused.

The smell of lotus blossoms wafted by my nose, the scent laden with citrus and mixed with an enticing hint of cinnamon. This was followed by the sweet smell of wet earth after a hard rain.

"I must admit," said the voice from behind me, "you certainly have a gift for pissing off beings that can destroy you. Are you trying to find out how immortal you are?"

"Hello, Karma." I moved back away from Slif. "I need to end this dragon. Any tips?"

She was dressed in a black, exercise one-piece that hugged each and every one of her curves. She wore matching sneakers and a half-top jacket that said BITCH on the back. I smiled despite myself.

"One suggestion would be not to engage in altercations with beings outside of your weight class? But we're past that part of the conversation," she said, looking around. "Your mage and your pet are down—so it's just you. And you drank the entire flask?"

I nodded. "Figured I'd go big or go home."

"Or get dead," she said, shaking her head. "Dragon

scale is mostly immune to magic. You have to find a way to negate that immunity. Then she can be vulnerable to any magical attack. Perhaps your blade?"

My time was almost up, but I had a plan. "Thank you," I said, exhaling and looking at Ebonsoul. "I didn't really expect to see you. I just needed a breather from the impending flash roasting."

"I don't know if I'll see you after this, Simon," she said, looking up at the dragon towering over us. "It was certainly interesting getting to know you if only for a short time. Goodbye."

I started running even before she faded away. I ran up Slif's back, buried Ebonsoul in her neck, and hung on. Out of the corner of my eye, I saw Monty. Time snapped back as Slif exhaled and blasted the area where I'd stood seconds earlier, melting concrete and asphalt.

"Monty, I need a Beck special!" I yelled from behind her. "Now would be good!"

He drew his lips together in a tight line and nodded.

He put his hands together in prayer fashion, and spoke. Slif turned her attention to him and was about to blast him when he released the largest orb of energy I had ever seen. I twisted Ebonsoul into her and broke through her scales.

The orb was easily the size of a large van, which was still miniature in comparison to a dragon. He said another word and it homed in on me. Slif raised a claw and impaled my shoulder. It was all I could do to stay conscious through the pain. She fixed me with one of her eyes.

"Got you, you pest," she said with satisfaction. "I'm

going to erase you and leave your smeared carcass on my body as a trophy. Did you really think your toy blade was going to hurt me? I barely feel it."

"First: that's just—ugh, that's disgusting. My carcass, really? Second: I just needed to get past your scales. You have incoming," I said as the orb raced at me.

She turned her head in time to see the black orb crash into us. Ebonsoul acted like what it was—a siphon. It channeled the orb of black energy into Slif as she whacked me off her shoulder and sent me flying. So much for being a smear. I think I was headed for "flattened" at the velocity I was traveling.

The wall rushed at me fast and then slowed as Monty hit me with a cushion of air. I still bounced off the wall, just not at bone-crushing speed. Peaches raced over to where I was and tugged at my arm, getting me on my feet unsteadily. I looked around and scrambled for Ebonsoul. I grabbed it and got my feet under me.

<We have to run. Can you run?>

I looked in Slif's direction, I saw her take another breath to incinerate us. Monty was already down the street.

"Simon, run!" he yelled as I pressed the bead on the mala, and the shield rose up.

Those were the last words I heard before the world erupted in flame.

THIRTY-NINE

"He should be dead, that's what he should be," said

another familiar voice. It was Corbel. "He was about ten feet away. How did he survive the dragon explosion?"

"It would seem that Mr. Strong is more resilient than he appears. Wouldn't you agree, Tristan?" Hades picked his way through the rubble. He wore a pristine black Stuart Hughes design without the diamonds. Piero would have a suitgasm if he saw Hades in that.

We were still in the street. I tried to sit up and the world swam away from me. So I laid my head down again until the world settled back into place. Peaches came over and licked my face.

<My saliva has healing properties,> he said when I winced.

"That's a lie," I muttered and pushed his huge head away.

<I know. You were just extra salty.> He bounded away to sit next to Monty. I just stared at him.

"Slif?" I croaked.

"Is dead," Monty said with a look of concern as he scanned up the street. "We still have work to do. She didn't have the artifacts and there is a small matter we need to attend to."

"Did you notice that I just got dragonploded down the street?"

"I also know your body is healing you even as we speak," he whispered, stepping close. "We have a tear to close before it's too late and we can't close it at all."

"I will have my people attend to your injured and fallen," Hades said and gestured with a hand. Several Valkyries stepped onto the street and moved toward Quan, Cassandra, and Davros.

"I may be healing, but there's no way I'm driving," I said as I wobbled to my feet. Peaches came over, stood next to me, steadying my leg.

"Corbel will drive you," Hades said. "You need to attend to this matter now before any other of my family develops an interest in the current state of affairs."

"That sounds bad. Why does that sound bad?" I said as Monty and Corbel led me to the Goat.

"Because it is." Corbel said, waiting while Monty opened the car. "If the other gods get involved, this will turn into a shitstorm of a magnitude you cannot comprehend."

I slid into the back seat and Peaches jumped in next to me and sprawled. I gave him a look and shoved his leg, which he promptly shoved back.

<This is my seat. I'm letting you share it with me. Now if you were a pretty lady…>

The roar of the engine filled the night as we took off. I looked through the rear window and Hades gave me a short nod before turning to the Valkyries.

By the time we arrived at 42nd Street, my body had dealt with the damage of the explosion. We raced down the streets and Corbel drove as if we were racing against the apocalypse. Monty had his eyes closed and was muttering something under his breath.

Corbel stopped the Goat with a lurch as the car skidded several feet. I rocked in my seat as the car came to a stop.

"Monty? I'm all for the teamwork and all that, but what am I doing here? It's not like I can help you close the vortex," I said as we got out of the Goat. "I don't use magic. Peaches, stay."

Monty narrowed his eyes. "I need your help. Over there. I need you to use your mark."

"My mark? But I'm the only one affected during its use. How is that going to help?"

"Do you really want me to explain the mechanics behind what I'm going to do?"

"Can't you do it in English I can understand?" I asked, walking over to where he indicated.

"Probably not."

"Try me," I said, looking for the tear but not seeing anything.

He slashed down with a hand and I saw the tear, a small vortex that seemed to be growing larger right before my eyes.

"I'm going to create another vortex around you," he started. I put my hands up and shook my head.

"Already not liking this plan. Can't you just close this one?" I stared at him and pointed at the vortex.

"I need an anchor who is immune to magic and can stop time. Do you know anyone else who can do what you do with the mark? If so, please refer them and Corbel will go pick them up."

"Fine, I'm your huckleberry. You need an immune anchor, and then?"

"When I tell you, you activate your mark. I will set off a negation spell and hopefully the two vortices will cancel each other out and leave you intact," he said, lowering his voice around the last part.

"Hopefully?" I stared at him, *hard*. "You've never done this before, have you? This is the first time you are attempting this and I get to be the guinea pig?" I said, my voice getting louder.

"The theory is sound. According to Ziller's theorem of magical gravity, the two vortices will collapse on each other and try to merge. That's when you'll stop time, and I will negate the process."

"I'm really disliking you right now," I said, taking a deep breath. "Fine. We don't have another choice. Let's get this done. I'm going on the record as saying this is the opposite of shaynetas—"

"You finish that sentence and I'll make sure there is an error somewhere in the casting process," he said seriously as he began to gesture. "Your immunity *should* keep you intact."

"I'd feel more confident if you had your staff. All this gesturing is beginning to look like spastic gang signs. The guy in Chicago doesn't use gang signs," I said quickly as the wind began to pick up. "He just points his staff and screams a word and *blam*—power. Even the other one in St. Louis doesn't need to shake his fingers all over the place. He just *thinks* and it happens. I'm starting to think mages need to improve on their casting abilities, but I guess you're a little old to catch a train at King's Cross."

"I understand your fear. It's this or deal with a missing city. Besides, logic clearly dictates that the needs of the many outweigh the needs of the few," He gave me a look with a tight smile.

"Or the one," I answered as he cast the vortex. "I have a really bad feeling about this. Corbel, you may want to move a little farther away in case Mage Montague gets this wrong."

Corbel jumped into the Goat and floored it. Peaches

looked out the back window as they drove away. Then he vanished.

"Um, Monty? Peaches just disappeared from the back seat."

"That creature vanishes all the time. This isn't a surprise. Now, when I tell you," he said, raising his voice as the wind picked up, "activate your mark."

He focused and as the vortex formed, I felt the tug of the wind. The magical forces within the vortex slid around me, but just couldn't quite grab hold. As the second vortex formed, they crept towards each other, unable to resist, like the opposite poles of a magnet. I felt the magical pressure like a solid weight on my chest, but that was the extent of its effect.

I saw what it was doing to Monty, though. His face was red with the effort, deep frown lines furrowed his brow, and his breath came in short, rasping gasps. Sweat poured down his brow and into his eyes. In that moment, I realized he was too close. If this failed, he would be sucked into the vortex with me. When I saw the blood, I seriously thought we weren't walking away from this one. Blood started trickling down his nose and out of the corner of his eyes. I saw him open his mouth but couldn't hear what he said.

"Now!" his voice crashed into me a few seconds later. It reminded me of the old kung fu movies where the dubbing never matched the movement of the lips.

I pressed the mark and everything grew hazy and out of focus. I saw him release a large black orb into the vortex, but nothing happened—for at least three seconds. Then I saw the vortex fray and break apart. One of them disappeared immediately. The second one was taking its time and I could feel it dragging me in.

Then I remembered: I'm not immortal when I use the mark, which meant my immunity was gone too. It was one of those 'oh shit' moments. Like when the door is about to lock and you realize the keys are inside the car just as the door closes. I tried signaling to Monty but he was losing it too. His nose was now gushing blood. He was visibly paling before me and he was increasingly unstable on his feet. It looked like we would both have that conversation with Ezra sooner than expected. The vortex was closing and pulling me down, when I felt a pressure punch me in the chest and sent me flying out of it.

Peaches was covered in runes like and resembled a light show. He pulled me away from the vortex by my arm and rushed back in, reappearing moments later and dragging a battered Monty by the arm. I turned to look back at the vortex as it winked out of existence. I heard the Goat in the distance followed by sirens, and then I passed out.

FORTY

"Stop it." I shoved my hands in front of me. "Stop giving me a bath."

<My saliva also has restorative properties. See how it brought you back?>

"Your saliva is just gross, but thank you for the save, boy," I said, giving him a hug. "Just cool it with the licking."

"This is a touching scene, really," Ramirez said as he stepped close to where I lay. "All that's missing is Lassie and the boy who fell down the well. Speaking of missing—where is my lieutenant?"

"Angel…" I said, and he knew. "I'm sorry."

"Fuck, Simon. What the fuck! So help me God, *you* are going to deliver the news to her father!" he yelled and stormed off. Everyone at the scene looked in my direction. The EMTe working on me remained silent.

I let him scream and walk away. He needed to process it, and we all did it in our own way. Ramirez did it with screaming and breaking things.

"You'd better go after him before he puts his hands through a windshield," I said to the EMTe next to me. I saw Frank come on the scene and I motioned to him. He had the unlit cigar in his mouth and chewed it as he approached. "Where's Monty?"

"He's in the unit. I don't know what you two were up to but he's stable now. He'll be on his way to Haven and Roxy in ten. You, on the other hand should be in a lab somewhere getting tested."

"No thanks, OG," I said and got to my feet. "It's been a long night."

"Suit yourself," he said, looking at me. "Listen, I ride you guys hard, but I know sometimes you're out here doing the things no one else can or wants to do. Thanks for that."

I put a hand to my chest. "That almost sounded like you cared. I'm touched."

"You're touched all right," he said and pointed to his head. "Right in the head."

"That's what I hear." I walked with Peaches by my

side to the ambulance that held Monty. "See you soon, Frank."

"See me soon? The DC looks like a bomb went off and this" —he looked around at the damage from the vortices and shook his head—"will take weeks to fix. I don't want to see you or your partner for a few months at least. I'm getting too old for this shit."

I jumped into the EMTe unit. It looked like a standard ambulance except for the runes covering the inside. They glowed faintly in the night as I looked at Monty. He was battered, bruised, and beaten. His face looked like he had gone a few rounds with a professional boxer. His eyes were swollen shut and his nose was about three times the normal size.

"Can I have a moment?" I said as the EMTe medic strapped Monty in. He stepped out with a sharp nod and held up one hand with the fingers splayed, letting me know I had five minutes. I nodded in return. "Hey, Monty. How're you feeling?" I whispered, crouching next to him.

"How do I look?" he answered, turning his head in the direction of my voice.

"Like a truck hit you—twice. Pretty bad."

"That's how I feel. The vortex?"

"It's closed. I saw it close. The city is safe." I patted him on the shoulder. "I'll meet you at Haven."

"It's not safe," he said and grabbed my hand. "Slif said 'we' so they're not done. Someone or something is behind this. We need to find them and stop them."

"You get to Haven and Roxanne," I said as I stood up. "Once you get back to one hundred percent, we can discuss hunting them down. I'll meet you at the hospital."

I jumped out of the unit as the EMTe medic climbed in the back and closed the door. The Goat was parked down the block. I saw Corbel standing next to it, and I made my way over to him.

"This is one sweet cruisemobile," he said with admiration in his voice. "Who did the rune work and how did they manage the large scale Ziller Effect?"

"Monty did. Said he wanted to make it safe," I said as I noticed Hades in the back seat. "You'll have to ask him about the zipper thing. He tried to explain it to me and nearly gave me an aneurysm."

"He wants to talk to you," Corbel said with a nod to Hades in the back. I opened the passenger side door and Peaches jumped in, rocking the Goat. I sat behind the wheel and closed the door. Corbel remained outside.

"I thought Chaos exploded you along with the building?" I said to break the ice. "How did you survive?"

He waved away my words. "Simon, many people died that day, but I wasn't one of them. The curse Kali placed on you is quite strong. You drank an entire flask of Hel's brew and still live to tell the tale."

"It's coffee. Really good coffee," I said, remembering the experience. "And it was probably one of the reasons I survived that dragon explosion. *You* said they didn't exist."

"Would you have believed me if I said they did?"

I glanced at him. "Coming from you? Probably not."

Hades looked at me for a few long seconds and then smiled. "Go tend to your friend. Tell him to prepare for a visit. The Golden Circle will call him to-task for opening not one, but *two* void vortices in a city," he said, looking at me in the rearview mirror. "Tell him to bury his friend and go home. There is much unrest in the Sanctuary."

"What about the dragons? Are they going to be pissed we exploded one of them?"

"Most certainly, but they will not act overtly. They prefer the long game, playing from the shadows. You can rest assured they will be watching the two of you. As for your fallen—the NYTF has the body of the lieutenant, and the Golden Circle will be retrieving the body of the mage."

"And Quan?"

"I'm sure you will be getting a visit from the mage soon. You have something she needs to recover," he said, leaning forward and placing two boxes on the front seat next to me. "One is for the grieving father, the other for the White Phoenix."

"I didn't get you anything. I didn't know we were exchanging gifts."

"Your humor never fails to amuse, Simon. Actually, you've given me more than you'll understand." He looked out the window. "You have a difficult conversation approaching. I *will* see you soon."

He exited the car and walked across the street to a waiting limousine. I recognized it as a SuNaTran vehicle, which meant it was a mini-tank disguised as a limo. He and Corbel got in and it pulled away, silently fading into the night.

I turned to see George 'Rottweiler' Rott walking my way. His posture and gait said military. He still wore a screaming-eagle cut and I noticed the pressed suit under the coat. I reached for the boxes as he closed in on me, grabbing the heavier one as I opened the door and got out.

"Strong," he said and held out his hand. I shook it and he went silent a moment, as if searching for the words. "How did she die? What killed her? What took my little girl down?"

"A dragon, sir."

"A dragon?" he said with the hint of sad smile. "Well shit, Cassie. Well done."

"We took care of the dragon," I said quickly.

"All of them?" he said, staring hard into my eyes. "Did you get them all?"

"No, sir. Just the one."

"I see," he said after a moment's pause.

"Sir, she went down swinging. She wanted me to give you this," I said and handed him the box.

He opened the lid and I saw his eyes glisten. Inside was his daughter's Magnum—the gift he had given her on her first day at the NYTF.

He cleared his throat. "Thank you. She wanted fieldwork. I told her of the danger, but she was a stubborn one. Took after her father," he said and his voice caught in his throat.

"I'm sorry for your loss, sir," I said and paused. "All she ever wanted was to make you proud."

"I've been proud of her from the day she was born," he said his voice filled with emotion. "We'll be in touch," he said and walked off into the night.

FORTY-ONE

I pulled up to Haven Medical and parked the Goat. I had the other box tucked under my arm as we left the parking lot. Peaches kept pace next to me and rumbled when I saw her.

<She is a fierce fighter. I like her. Can I give her a small bite?>

"No, don't bite her. Not even a friendly one," I whispered as Quan approached us. "Hello, Quan."

She bowed, placing one hand in front of her chest with the knife-edge facing me. I returned the bow. She crouched down and rubbed Peaches on the head as I held my breath, hoping she would keep her hand.

"Hello, Simon," she said, looking at the box under my arm. "I must return to my sect before the Golden Circle arrives. There has been some tension. I don't wish to escalate it. May I have it?"

I held out the box that held the Phoenix Tail and gave it to her. She took it with both hands and bowed again. "Please take care of him. You are a good friend. He is fortunate to have you all."

"Are you coming up to see him? I'm sure he would want to know you're okay."

She shook her head with a sad smile. "No, it's best this way. He knows I'm safe the same way I know he's safe. We are connected. Sometimes words are inadequate." She looked up to the windows. "Besides, another love fills his heart now."

She traced a rune, and a circle appeared in the

ground. I recognized it from the Hellfire. It was a teleportation circle.

"Goodbye, Simon. I hope the next time we meet it will be under happier circumstances." She stepped into the circle and disappeared.

<You should have let me bite her.>

I rubbed his head. "I'll get you a titanium chew toy. You can bite that all you want. Let's go see Monty."

THE END

CAST OF CHARACTERS FOR FULL MOON HOWL

Allen Montgomery-Medical Examiner for the NYTF. Specializes in supernatural autopsies. Liaison for the OCME and the NYTF. If Allen hasn't seen it, it doesn't exist.

Andrei Belyakov-Olga's eyes and ears at The Moscow. He handles the day-to-day affairs of the building and reports to Olga. Has an instinctual self-preserving fear of Peaches.

Angel Ramirez-Director of the NYTF and friend to Simon Strong. Cannot believe how much destruction one detective agency can wage in the course of one day.

Beck Sinclair-Negomancer who works for the Dark Council. Responsible for erasures-magical and physical.

Cathain Grobjorn-Hel's brewer of Valhalla Java.

Producer of the Odinforce blend-drink of the heroes of Valhalla. Any mortal that drinks this blend has Death Wish since it is fatal to humans.

Cassandra Rott- Daughter of George Rott. Lieutenant in the NYTF under Director Angel Ramirez.

Cecil Fairchild-Owner of SuNaTran and close friend of Tristan Montague. Provides transport for the supernatural community and has been known to make a vehicle disappear in record time.

Corbel Nwobon-(AKA the 'Hound of Hades') Enforcer of the Underworld. Occasionally smells of fire and brimstone from frequent visits to the Underworld.

Davros Dahlech- One of the *Ordarum*. Mage of the Golden Circle who was erased and incarcerated for war crimes and mental instability.

Erik Rothsfeld- Director of the Hellfire Club in NYC. Sitting Mage Representative on the Dark Council.

Ezrael-(AKA Ezra, Azrael-the Angel of Death, Death, Thanatos, Big D) the personification of Death. Feared, disliked, and respected by human and supernatural alike. Loves pastrami on rye and sitting in his favorite deli on 1st Avenue studying when he isn't out "collecting" or in his office at Arkangel Industries.

Georgianna Wittenbraden-Vampire of a powerful clan who is currently shunned and being assisted by the Montague & Strong Detective Agency.

George "Rottweiler" Rott- Retired NYTF Special Ops leader. Father of Cassandra Rott.

The Hack-Cybercriminal, security expert, and

friend of Simon. He is feared and hunted by every three-letter agency on the planet. If it's digital it's at risk.

Hades-Ruler of the Underworld. Rules the dead and is generally seen around funerals and wakes. Favorite song by the Eagles is 'Hotel California'-especially that part about checking out, but never leaving.

Hel- Norse version of Hades with a mean streak and extra pain.

Ken Nakatomi-Michiko's brother and elite assassin for the Dark Council. If you're his target and you see him-it's the last thing you ever see.

Kali-(AKA Divine Mother) goddess of Time, Creation, Destruction, and Power. Cursed Simon for unspecified reasons and has been known to hold a grudge. She is also one of the most powerful magic-users in existence.

Karma-The personification of causality, order, and balance. She reaps what you sow. Also known as the mistress of bad timing. Everyone knows the saying karma is a…some days that saying is true.

Michiko Nakatomi-(AKA 'Chi' if you've grown tired of breathing) Vampire leader of the Dark Council. Reputed to be the most powerful vampire in the Council.

Noh Fan Yat- Martial arts instructor for the Montague & Strong Detective Agency. Teacher to both Simon and Tristan. Known for his bamboo staff of pain and correction.

Olga Etrechenko-Simon's landlord and current owner of The Moscow. She has an uncanny ability for tracking Simon down when the rent is due. You never cheat Olga.

Peaches-(AKA Devildog, Hellhound, Arm Shredder and Destroyer of Limbs) Offspring of Cerberus and given to the Montague & Strong Detective Agency to help with their security. Closely resembles a Cane Corso.

Piero Roselli-Vampire and owner of Roselli's-an upscale restaurant and club that caters to the supernatural community. If Piero doesn't seat you, you aren't staying.

Quan Toh-Mage of the White Phoenix sect. Master healer and past ally of Tristan. Shares an *umbra mortis* bond to prevent Tristan going dark. Dangerous, deadly and slightly deranged.

Roxanne DeMarco-Director of Haven. Oversees both the Medical and Detention Centers of the facility. Is an accomplished sorceress with formidable skill. Has been known to make Tristan stammer and stutter with merely a touch of his arm.

Simon Strong-The intelligent (and dashingly handsome) half of the Montague & Strong Detective Agency. Cursed alive into immortality by the goddess Kali.

Slif- Ancient Dragon working to undo the spread of magic among non-dragonkind.

Tristan Montague- The civilized (and staggeringly brilliant) half of the Montague & Strong Detective Agency. Mage of the Golden Circle sect and currently on 'extended leave' from their ever-watchful supervision.

White Phoenix-An ancient sect of Mages

comparable to the Golden Circle. Emphasis on physical magic use and healing.

William Montague- Brother to Tristan Montague. Reported deceased-location unknown.

Yama-Assigned bodyguard to Georgianna. A personal guard of Michiko Nakatomi. He is known to exhibit dizzying heights of eloquence in grunts and stares.

ORGANIZATIONS

Christye, Blahq, &Doil-Law firm that shares the same floor with the Montague & Strong Detective Agency. Never seem to be open, but always ready for business.

New York Task Force-(AKA the NYTF) a quasi-military police force created to deal with any supernatural event occurring in New York City.

SuNaTran-(AKA Supernatural Transportations) Owned by Cecil Fairchild. Provides car and vehicle service to the supernatural community in addition to magic-users who can afford membership.

The Dark Council- Created to maintain the peace between humanity and the supernatural community shortly after the last Supernatural War. Its role is to be a check and balance against another war occurring. Not everyone in the Council favors peace.

AUTHOR NOTES

Thank you for reading this story and jumping back into the world of Monty & Strong. Tombyards & Butterflies was an absolute blast to write. That made writing this book easy and hard. I wanted to make sure it did justice to the first book and yet I wanted to introduce you to different elements of the world Monty & Strong inhabit. Let me know if I pulled it off.

There are some references you may get and some… you may not. This may be attributable to my age (I'm older than Monty) or to my love of all things sci-fi and fantasy. As a reader, I've always enjoyed finding these "Easter Eggs" in the books I read. I hope you do too. If there is a reference you don't get feel free to email me and I will explain it…maybe.

You will notice that Simon is still a smart-ass (deserving a large head smack) and many times he's clueless about what's going on. Bear with him—he's still new to the immortal, magical world he's been delicately shoved into. Fortunately he has Monty to nudge (or blast) him in the right direction.

Each book will reveal more about Monty& Strong's backgrounds and lives before they met. Rather than hit you with a whole history, I wanted you to learn about them slowly, the way we do with a person we just met —over time (and many cups of coffee).

Thank you for taking the time to read this book. I wrote it for you and I hope you enjoyed spending a few more hours getting in (and out of) trouble with Tristan and Simon.

If you really enjoyed this story, I need you to do me a HUGE favor— **Please leave a review**.

It's really important and helps the book (and me). Plus it means Peaches gets more chew toys, besides my arms, legs, and assorted furniture to shred and we want to keep Peaches happy, don't we?

I really do appreciate your feedback. Let me know what you thought by emailing me at:
www.orlando@orlandoasanchez.com

For more information on Monty & Strong...come join the MoB on Facebook!
You can find us at:
Montague & Strong Case Files.

To get FREE books visit my page at:
www.orlandoasanchez.com

Still here? Amazing! Well, if you have made it this far —you deserve something special!
Included is the first chapter of the next Montague & Strong story-BLOOD IS THICKER here for you to read. Enjoy!

BLOOD IS THICKER

Montague & Strong Book 3
"You did thirst for blood, and with blood I fill you."-

Dante Alighieri, Inferno

ONE

A biting wind cut across the water as we landed on North Brother Island. We stepped off the ferry and onto the slick, deserted dock. The dawn rain pelted my face until Monty gestured and formed a shield around us, stopping the cold droplets from landing.

Peaches, fearing I might be too dry, shook the water off his body, drenching me but somehow missing Monty.

"Really? Thank you," I said with a groan. "It's not like I was soaked or anything."

<This water is cold and I don't like being wet.>

"You need to lay off the pastrami, and then you would have less surface area," I said, looking down at him as we walked. He appeared to be a Cane Corso, but was really the offspring of Cerberus, minus the three heads. He stepped close to me and kept pace as we walked off the dock and onto a short boardwalk. The boards creaked under his weight as he padded by my side.

<Are you saying I'm getting fat?>

"There's no *getting* about it. You sound like you're going to break through the boardwalk. Maybe Ezra has a low-fat pastrami option."

<Low–fat? Those words are sacrilege. Pastrami and all related meats are essential for my wellbeing, and the safety of humankind. Speaking of which, are we going to eat soon?>

"I told you to stay home, but you wanted to come," I said, ignoring his nudge into my leg. "We'll swing by Ezra's on the way back—you can eat then."

A low rumble was his response as we kept walking.

"Are you talking to your creature again?" Monty said looking at me. "You need to find a less overt method of communication. One that doesn't make you appear as insane as you are."

I patted Peaches on the head. "Everyone talks to their dogs. It's even therapeutic and healing."

"Everyone talks *to* their dogs not *with*, and that" — he glanced at Peaches—"barely qualifies as part of the *dog species*." Monty held a small wooden box and looked farther inland. He narrowed his eyes and pointed. "That way."

"I didn't even know these islands existed." I pulled my coat tighter against the elements. Monty seemed unaffected by the rain and wind. "Are you sure he's here? She could have lied. Dragons aren't known for their honesty."

"We checked the South Island, and his energy is in the vicinity. Check the device again."

The Hack, after recovering from nearly losing Manhattan to a black hole, had finally answered my calls. I assured him the city wasn't going to disappear in some cataclysm and he'd grudgingly provided me with his latest 'magical tech.'

He called it a runic filter. It was designed to detect spikes in magical energy. It could distinguish between ambient energy and magical energy in any given environment, according to the Hack. It looked like a smartphone, only thicker. I pressed on the screen. Three blips showed up on the topographical map of the island.

"Monty, I think we have a problem." I showed him

the screen. "Which one of those is your brother?"

"The dragon lied," he said with a smile. He examined the filter closer. "This is actually good news."

"Why am I not surprised?" I said, handing him the filter. "Do you think she even saw your brother or was it all smoke? And, excuse me, good news?"

He nodded and pushed some hair out of his face. "I don't know the purpose of Slif's deceit. What I do know is that these mages are quite powerful." He closed his eyes. "They must have found a way to replicate William's energy signature."

"And this is good news because...?" I said, confused. "Wait, how do you know they're mages?"

"It's good news because there's a possibility William is still alive. I know what they are because I can sense them irrespective of this device" —he held up the runic filter—"and it seems we're here to have a conversation."

"Shit, can we just go back the way we came and avoid this *conversation*?" I said, shaking my head. "They never end well, mostly because they're heavy on the fireballs and light on the actual conversing."

"How did they mimic William's energy signature?" he said, rubbing his chin and handing me back the filter. "They must possess something of his with a recent imprint. It's the only way they could have created such a powerful signature."

We arrived at the only standing structure on the island. It was an abandoned hospital erected at the turn of the nineteenth century to deal a smallpox outbreak. The building was partially intact. Trees and undergrowth had reclaimed most of the property. In front of the hospital, a circle roughly fifty feet in diameter had been cleared away. Covered in runes, it held a small pulsing orb in the center.

"That looks recent," I said, pointing at the circle before looking around into the trees. I pressed the runic filter again, but it came up blank. "Looks like they left. Maybe they got tired of waiting for you?"

"Unlikely." He narrowed his eyes as he looked around. "I still sense them. They must be close."

Three figures materialized inside the cleared circle. They wore black robes with deep hoods that covered their faces. Each of the robes was trimmed in gold brocade. A large golden circle rested on the chest of each.

Peaches dropped into a 'pounce and maim' posture and rumbled next to me. He lowered his head and spread his forepaws, the muscles of his back rippling with anticipation.

"Golden Circle police?" I asked as I opened my jacket to give me easier access to my weapons. "The 'dark and ominous' thing works well for them."

"Envoys—messengers sent to escort rogue mages back to the Sanctuary," Monty said, and shook out one hand. "Usually by force."

The Envoy in the center stepped forward and pushed back his hood. A look of recognition crossed Monty's face. The Envoy appeared to be in his mid-thirties. His long blond hair was tied back in a ponytail. He gave me a cursory glance and let his dark eyes settle on Monty with a look of disappointment.

"Friend of yours?" I asked, taking a step back and letting my hand rest on Grim Whisper. "I get the impression he doesn't like what he sees."

"Gideon, I see you've been made an Envoy," Monty said with a nod. "When I left, you were still an apprentice. How are you?"

"Better than you," Gideon answered and formed an orb of fire in his hand. The two Envoys next to him did the same.

"Why do mages always default to fireballs?" I whispered under my breath, drawing Grim Whisper. "They don't seem in the *conversing* mood, Monty."

Monty took a step forward and flexed his hands. Gideon extended his other hand and formed a second fireball. "Don't do this, Gideon."

Gideon allowed the orbs in his hand to float lazily in front of him. "Mage Tristan Montague, by order of the Elders of the Golden Circle, you are hereby instructed to surrender yourself to the custody of the Envoys. You will be returned to the Sanctuary to await judgment for the crime of casting a forbidden spell—a void vortex—in a populated area."

"And if I refuse?" Monty asked, keeping his eyes on Gideon while placing the box he was holding on the ground.

"Then we are authorized to use deadly force to carry out our mandate." Gideon entered a defensive stance. "Don't make me hurt you, Tristan."

Thank You!

If you enjoyed this book, would you please help
me by leaving a review at the site where you
purchased it from? It only needs to be a sentence
or two and it would really help me out a lot!

All of My Books

The Warriors of the Way
The Karashihan* • Spiritual Warriors • The Ascendants
• The Fallen Warrior • The Warrior Ascendant • The
Master Warrior

John Kane
The Deepest Cut* • Blur

Sepia Blue
The Last Dance* • Rise of the Night

Chronicles of the Modern Mystics
The Dark Flame • A Dream of Ashes

Montague & Strong Detective Agency
Tombyards & Butterflies - Full Moon Howl

**Books denoted with an asterisk are FREE via
my website.*
www.OrlandoASanchez.com

ACKNOWLEDGMENTS

I'm finally beginning to understand that each book, each creative expression usually has a large group of people behind it. This book is no different. So let me take a moment to acknowledge my (very large) group:

To Dolly: my wife and biggest fan. You make all of this possible and keep me grounded, especially when I get into my writing to the exclusion of everything else. Thank you, I love you.

To my Tribe: You are the reason I have stories to tell. You cannot possibly fathom how much and how deep I love you all.

To Lee: Because you were the first audience I ever had. I love you sis.

To the Logsdon family: JL you saw the script and pushed me to bring my A-game and flesh it out into a story. LL your notes and comments turned this story from good to great.

Your patience knows no bounds. Thank you both.

Arigatogozaimasu

<u>To my Launch Team</u>: Dolly S. Steve L. Bill T. Mark R. Leslie P. Tracy B.

MaryAnn S. Chris S. Jonathan G. Penny C-M. Derek C. Tammy B. Angie H. Kate. John P L.(Author Guru Extraordinaire) Rachel S. Darren. David S.

Bryan G. Michelle S. Kerry. Brian R. Melissa K. Katy L. Jim Z. Marie McC. Jeff B. Carrie O'L. Bill H. Carmen E. Leigh Ann M. Channah H.(Blurb Jedi). Chris P. Cheryl. Cassandra H. Myles C. Terry B. Lorella. Lawrence G. Wayne G. P Sophie.

<u>ART-Group</u>

(In no particular order)

EricCandace, Carrie, Thomas, Brenda,

Timothy,Frederick,Cassandra,Penny,Tracy,
Maryann,Bill,Isabel,Elena,Mae,

Christopher,Stephanie,Joscelyn,Marie,Darre
n.Sue,Amanda,Charlotte,Mary,Claudine,

Karla,Julie,Amy,Bernice,Lynne,Eliz-
sha,TracyB.,Davina,Natalie,Amy
Beth,Elizabeth,Mandy Pants,MaryAnn

You took on reading my (very) rough draft
and helped me polish it into something
resembling a legible book. YOU GUYS
ROCK!

<u>The Montague & Strong Case Files</u>
<u>Group AKA- The MoB(The Mages of</u>

<u>BadAssery)</u>

When I wrote T&B there were fifty-five members in The MoB. As of this writing there are 156 members in the MoB. I am honored to be able to call you my MoB Family.

You all withstood the torture of snippets(lol) and shared your insights into the characters, the story and other ideas(still looking at you, Jim) that sometimes my brain was not caffeinated enough for. Thank you for being part of this group and M&S. You each make it possible.

THANK YOU.

<u>Special Mentions</u>

On occasion, in the course of writing the book and our daily conversations some of you have shared some incredible ideas, thoughts and insights. Most of these make it into the current book in some way shape or form. Somehow my twisted brain takes it and reworks it. These mentions go out to those who have influenced my thought process.

Jim-for the brain melting pre and post coffee conversations

Bonni-For the trip through the magical forest of Ash, Rowan,and Yew. (Plus COFFEE!!)

Kate-Because Karma can be a bitch, but not YOUR bitch. That was excellent.

Carrie-I don't know how many energy drinks it took…but thank you!! (GAME ON!)

Davina(AKA the Comma Ninja) who knew I was so allergic to commas? You did.

Kane and Sierra@Death Wish Coffee-for fueling the evenings, morning, (and afternoons) of frenzied activity with Valhalla Java-The Coffee of Valkyries! Thank you for letting me use your amazing coffee in the book.

Michael and everyone over at 20Books to 50K. Your selfless sharing and motivation was key in my having a strong community of readers.

I'm sure I missed some, but I will be taking notes from now on.

TEA-The English Advisory

(they needed a posh name, being English and all)

Aaron, Penny, Carrie

This small but select group advised me on all things English. Since I wasn't born in the UK they helped with ideas regarding Monty's speech and behavior. If Monty seems to be authentically English it's due to this group…Cheers!

WTA-The Incorrigibles

JL,BenZ, EricQK, S.S., and Mac

They sound like a bunch of badass misfits because they are. Thank you for making sure I didn't rush this one. My exposure to the slightly deranged and extremely deviant brain trust that you are made this book possible. I humbly thank you and it's all your fault.

Deranged Doctor Design

Kim, Darja, and Milo

You define professionalism and creativity. Thank you for the great service and amazing covers.

YOU GUYS RULE!

<u>To you the reader:</u>

Thank you for jumping down the rabbit hole with me. I truly hope you enjoy this story. You are the reason I wrote it.

ABOUT THE AUTHOR

Orlando Sanchez has been writing ever since his teens when he was immersed in creating scenarios for playing Dungeon and Dragons with his friends every weekend. An avid reader, his influences are too numerous to list here. Some of the most prominent are: J.R.R. Tolkien, Jim Butcher, Kat Richardson, Terry Pratchett, Christopher Moore,Terry Brooks, Piers Anthony, Lee Child, George Lucas, Andrew Vachss, and Barry Eisler to name a few in no particular order.

The worlds of his books are urban settings with a twist of the paranormal lurking just behind the scenes and generous doses of magic, martial arts, and mayhem.

Aside from writing, he holds a 2nd and 3rd Dan in two distinct styles of Karate. If not training, he is studying some aspect of the martial arts or martial arts philosophy.

He currently resides in Queens, NY with his wife and children and can often be found in the local Starbucks where most of his writing is done.

Please visit his site at OrlandoASanchez.com for more information about his books and upcoming releases.